Searching
for
Murder

Dedicated to Tom Hovet,
a magnificent teacher and friend
—and consummate search committee member.

* * *

Special thanks to Roy Arnold, Gary Beach, John Byrne,
Jan Holcomb, Linda Hosek, and Bill Wilkins.

PART ONE

A Perfect Place to Kill Someone
June 12, 2005

"He who enters a university walks on hallowed ground."

—James Bryant Conant

Of all the archaic customs and rituals still followed at major universities, commencement makes the most sense. Once a year, the entire university community gathers to send its students out into the world. It is, as most dictionaries define it, "a formal beginning."

But it accomplishes much more because it is also an ending to the academic year, the day everyone waits for from September onward. The university also pauses to honor noted alumni and distinguished people from the outside by giving them honorary degrees and distinguished service awards.

I also like the ceremony because of all the pomp associated with it; my mother suggested that was because of our English ancestry. For me, wearing a black robe and a hood on a hot afternoon just before the beginning of summer was not torture. It was something expected of me as a faculty member.

In my early years on the journalism faculty, I participated whenever a student I was especially proud of was graduating.

In recent years, I served as a faculty marshal, helping to organize the students in the College of Liberal Arts into the proper order so they would get the diplomas with their own names on them while on the stage. To do so meant an extraordinary effort behind the scenes by the staff of the Registrar's Office to pull out the diplomas of the students who chose not to attend—usually, as students tend to do everything, at the last minute. Their reward for all this hard work was the smiles of students who grabbed their diplomas on the stage, glanced at the name, and started smiling immediately. That moment of victory was also shared by the hundreds of parents, grandparents, brothers and sisters, and spouses in the audience. Many of them had sacrificed mightily to help pay tuition and other costs during the years of study for their student.

That is the true meaning of commencement. But tradition plays as important a role as to why Oregon University—or any other institution of higher learning—goes through the annual ritual.

Commencement ceremonies go back as far as the Middle Ages. In that period, robes now worn by faculty members and students today were a common form of dress. The caps, which were originally round, later became square and came to be known as mortar boards. The hoods attached to the gowns were originally cowls like those still worn by monks, as a protection from bad weather.

Sleeves and hoods identify both the degree held by the wearer and the field of study. A bachelor's gown has pointed sleeves, the master's gown long closed sleeves. The doctor's gown has bell-shaped sleeves and velvet trim. The colored velvet border of the hood indicates the field of study to which the degree pertains, as do the tassel colors.

The colored lining of the hood indicates the institution from which the person wearing it received a degree. For example, the lining color for Harvard University is crimson, while Yale is blue; California is gold and Wisconsin, bright red. The color for Oregon University is burnt orange.

This year I was at commencement in a different role—I was here to babysit the three finalists to become the new university president. As secretary of the committee conducting this nationwide search, it was just one of the hundreds of details I had needed to attend to over the past year. It was unusual for three candidates to be on campus at the same time. It was not unusual that I—or someone in a similar position of responsibility—would see to the details.

In its long search, the committee had narrowed down its list to these three people, and they were in town to "run the gauntlet" for the top job. Although slightly more humane than the presidential primary system, that set by the university was no less exhausting and challenging for those involved.

I was at the football stadium the day before the ceremony to check the arrangements. The ceremony had been moved in recent years to this location from the basketball coliseum next door because of the increase in graduates. I preferred the intimacy of the basketball court—if a basketball court can be considered intimate—to the vast playing field of the football stadium, but this had not been my decision. I glanced across at the unfinished section of the stadium, which had been under construction for a year.

"Tom Martindale. What are you doing way down there?"

I looked up at the skyboxes high above. Like the elongated body of a praying mantis, these mini-apartments dwarfed the stands below them. They were a credit to the fundraisers who sold their use to corporations and fat-cat alumni for outrageous sums. Students and mere mortal fans had to sit in the stands below during the rains that usually hit Oregon halfway through the football season.

"Hi, Angela. I'll be right up."

Angela Pride and I had been, in the words of my beloved late grandmother, "keeping company" on and off for years. We like one another well enough to date and hop into bed together now and again, but not to commit to anything more permanent. I was rapidly reaching the age (fifty-five!) where I was too set in my ways to get married. I also spent most of my time teaching, writing, and lately, trying to keep the search committee headed in the right direction. Angela was similarly focused on doing her best as the head of campus security at OU and, presumably, advancing in rank and responsibility in the Oregon State Police, the state agency she really worked for.

As I climbed the stairs to the top of the stadium, I noticed that Angela was not alone. I recognized the tall, lean person standing beside her.

Paul Bickford and I had met the year before in the Arctic. I signed on as the public affairs man for an Arctic expedition studying ice; he was in charge of security. After a group of renegade Russians tried to take over the group in order to get the ice data, Bickford helped rescue me and the other people who survived a harrowing ordeal during which several people died.

I had found out enough about Bickford during our time together to know that he was more than a mere security consultant hired to keep greenhorn scientists from freezing to death. I knew he was a member of an elite special ops force with experience in Afghanistan, Iraq, and a hundred other trouble spots. I also knew that his predilection for secrecy usually caused him to hide his true identity.

"Tom Martindale. I'd like you to meet Major Paul Bickford of the United States Army."

"Professor Martindale. Good to meet you. Lieutenant Pride has been telling me all about you." Bickford shook his head imperceptibly and put out his hand. I took my cue from that.

"Major." I grasped his hand firmly and shook it. "Welcome to Oregon University. Good to meet you."

"Let's go up into the president's box so we can talk in more comfortable surroundings," said Angela.

Bickford and I followed Angela down an aisle and then up a stairway to an enclosed hall. We might have been in a luxury hotel or a passageway on an ocean liner. It certainly did not feel like we were in a football stadium.

Angela used a key to open a door, and we followed her inside. We entered the upper part of the box—a combination living room, dining room, and kitchen. Below us, down some steps, were several rows of theatre-style seats facing the all-glass wall above the playing field. The glass panels slid open so the box guests could hear as well as see the game on the field below. But that was not really necessary, given the presence of a number of television monitors situated around the room.

"Sit down, and I'll pour us some coffee."

Bickford and I sat down at a table that looked as though it belonged in an upscale home. Angela filled three cups from a stainless steel urn with coffee that she had obviously prepared earlier. She carried them over to us on a tray that also held a plate of cookies.

"Black, major?"

Bickford nodded and picked up the cup nearest him. He ignored the cookies. I snared a cookie along with my coffee, which Angela knew from long experience that I liked black. She sat down between us.

"I wanted the two of you to meet because we all have similar security concerns for the ceremony tomorrow. Why don't you tell Professor Martindale why you are on campus?"

Anyone who knew anything at all about the military could tell that Paul Bickford was a soldier. From his close-cropped hair to his ramrod straight posture to his tendency to call people even younger than him "sir" or "ma'am," he was every inch military. Even his civilian suit seemed more pressed. His shoes were so shiny that the bright lights of the skybox reflected off the toes.

"Yes, ma'am. I will be glad to." Bickford turned to me. "Sir, I am here because the commencement speaker is General John C. Chang, chairman of the Joint Chiefs of Staff. That high-profile job puts him in a vulnerable enough position to require extra security precautions on our part. But he is also a minority—Chinese-American as his name indicates. Also, he was my commanding officer in the Special Operations Command. Our enemies in this on-going war on terror have sworn to kill members of the military at all levels of command. He's about as high as you can get. They also have a special hatred for the Special Operations forces. You know, we put them on the run out of Afghanistan in 2001 and 2002."

"Before you all got sidetracked in Iraq," I added, helpfully and politically.

"No politics, please, Tom," said Angela.

"I'm not at liberty to comment on that, sir," added Bickford.

"I'll bet you aren't. Did you serve in Afghanistan, major?"

"I'm not at liberty to comment on that either, sir."

Before I could continue to needle Bickford, Angela intervened. "Gentlemen, I think we need to get back to our primary purpose here," she said. "Don't you agree?"

Bickford took that as a cue to continue his briefing. "We have no particular intelligence that terrorists are targeting your commencement ceremony or General Chang, beyond that earlier vow to kill members of the military."

"Do any terrorists actually live in the state?" I asked skeptically.

"I'm not at liberty to comment on that, sir," he replied. "We did have one instance in 1999 where a known al-Qaida leader was sent to establish a training course in the south Oregon desert near the town of Bly. That was in the news. It could happen again, I have no doubt."

"But it has not," I said.

"Tom, you're not being helpful here," said Angela. "This line of banter really has nothing to do with anything but your political agenda."

She was correct, of course. I was being a jerk. "You're right, Angela, I was out of line. Please continue, major." It seemed odd to be so formal, but we did have to keep up the fiction that we had just met.

"Thank you, sir. Because of General Chang's position and high rank, we will be providing him with both visible and plainclothes protection throughout the stadium, including the new section across the way."

Bickford gestured toward the playing field as he spoke. We all took in the scene: four large square towers to support the large steel structure that would be a mirror image to this side, a huge gantry crane to aid in construction, and the beginnings of steps and level areas where the seats would be. Here and there, huge steel girders protruded out from under the roof in a haphazard arrangement. The new part of the stadium looked impressive and dangerous. I shuddered as I thought about someone becoming impaled on one of those long steel spikes sticking out of the concrete towers, or falling the equivalent of twelve stories to certain death.

As we looked out of the large windows of the skybox, I realized how impossible it would be to stop a determined nutcase from wreaking havoc on thousands of unsuspecting faculty, students, and family members.

"We are beefing up our usual number of troopers that day as well," added Angela. "Your guests and the president's party should be perfectly safe."

"I don't doubt that for a moment," I said. "Do we have any reason to fear that one of our candidates is a target?"

"Not that I could find using our own intelligence database augmented by the FBI," said Angela.

"I am still checking out the names I was given," said Bickford. "Nothing is turning up so far."

"Do you expect it to?" I asked.

"If I knew the answer to that, professor, I could retire and write my memoirs."

"Sure, no way to know," I mumbled, feeling that I had been put in my place once again.

"Very well, then, I guess we have that all worked out," said Angela. "Do you have those photos I asked you to bring, Tom?"

I reached into my briefcase to retrieve double sets of shots of the three candidates who would be at commencement, and I handed them to her. She glanced at them briefly, kept one of each, and handed the others to Bickford.

"Our men will memorize these and keep a sharp eye out for anything untoward," he said.

"Our people will do the same," added Angela.

We got up and Angela motioned for us to follow her down the stairs to the front of the skybox.

"The formal academic procession will enter down that ramp to the left. First you'll see bagpipers, then the color guard, the chief marshal, the president and his party, and then everyone else. It takes at least a half-hour for them all to get in their seats. It's quite a sight."

"It always brings a lump to my throat," I said.

"We have checked out and sealed the entrances to all the rooftops along the procession route," said Bickford. "We'll have the personnel in place here that I already mentioned."

"Your people will already be in their seats in the president's box by then," said Angela, turning to me and holding up the ID photos. "Why aren't they marching?"

"It was felt that it would send too many mixed messages to the campus," I said. "We can only have one president at a time, and he will be out front, walking with General Chang."

"Okay, that makes sense. Any other questions?" said Angela. We both shook our heads.

"Very well. We'll hope for a successful and peaceful ceremony tomorrow."

Bickford and I raised our coffee cups in mock salute. The three of us climbed the stairs to the rear of the skybox.

"I'll stay behind and tidy up," said Angela, taking our cups from us and putting them back on the tray with the remaining cookies.

Bickford and I shook hands with her and each other before stepping out into the hall. We had walked to the elevator before either of us said a word.

"Why in the hell were you busting my balls in there, Tom?" he asked, as we descended to the main floor. "I was only trying to save your ass, yet again."

"Yeah, yeah, yeah. Don't I know it," I laughed. We walked toward the parking lot, still talking. "I've got a hundred questions about how you got out of the Arctic. I mean, the last time I saw you, you were chasing after a bunch of cowardly Russian

Commandos wearing heavy-duty winter gear." Bickford held up a hand to stop me from saying more. "Do you ever do anything like normal people—like have dinner? I'd even pay. We are friends, you know."

Bickford smiled slightly, then shook his head. "I've got to go over some background material tonight, then get ready to greet the general and his party out at the airport—or what passes for an airport here."

"Okay, okay. I didn't expect you to take me up on that offer. Where are you staying?"

"If I told you that, I'd have to kill you." Bickford said that with a casual deadpan expression, then broke into an uncharacteristic grin. Then, he did something very unexpected for him— he gave me one of those manly, pat-on-the-back hugs. As we were embracing, I looked up to see Angela gazing rather quizzically down at us from high above on the stadium upper level.

Commencement day dawned bright and clear, although the weatherman promised it would be warmer than usual. This would be true especially on the stadium floor. I was glad I was not marching in full—and suffocating—academic regalia.

After eating a quick breakfast at home, I drove to campus and parked near the stadium. Then I walked across the street to the Alumni Center where all the important people would be gathering in about an hour for coffee, sweet rolls, and small talk. Assistants from the University Special Events office were on hand to help special guests put on their robes and hoods. I wondered to myself if Bickford had added bulletproof panels inside of General Chang's robe.

I wandered down to a lounge on the main floor to go over the various schedules for the day and drink some coffee. In a few moments, my boss on this project, Hadley Collins, walked in. Since she was vice president for university relations, she had asked me to take on this assignment.

"Good morning, Hadley. You look very impressive and kind of sexy in that slinky gown."

"You say that to all the girls, I'm sure, Tom."

We embraced, and she sat down opposite me. "Big day, bigger number of headaches," she moaned. "It never gets any easier."

I started to speak, and she held up her hand. "You don't want to know."

"I think I've got my part taken care of. I got a security briefing yesterday afternoon from Angela Pride of the state police squad here on campus and Major Paul Bickford, an Army security specialist who is in charge of seeing that General Chang gets out of here unscathed."

She smiled. "That hardly seems much of a concern."

"I told him that, but they are worried that a terrorist might follow him to our campus in the hopes of finding everyone a bit lax."

"I don't suppose they can take anything for granted these days," she said. "How's the candidate search going? Even though I'm nominally vice-chairman, I've been too busy to attend many meetings. I'm counting on you to fill me in."

"We've narrowed it down to three candidates. They've all been here before, but we asked them to come back for more interviews."

"Odd to have them all here at the same time."

"Very odd and very unfortunate. It was a matter of scheduling. They are busy people, as you can well imagine. We had to take them when we could get them, and when we could get them is this weekend and the first few days of next week. Since they are here, it was the polite thing to do to invite them to attend today's events. We gave them a choice, and all three wanted to come."

"It's a good way to get into the rhythm of the place. Before long, they might be setting the pace for all of us."

"You can say that again," I said.

"I assume they'll want to be kept out of a spotlight," she said.

"You bet. No publicity of any kind. They are just to be faces in the crowd at all these events."

Hadley glanced at her watch, a look of alarm of her face. "I need to be in two places right about now." She got up to leave.

"Thanks, as always, Tom. It puts me at ease when you're in charge of something I've got the ultimate responsibility for."

"My pleasure—I think," I laughed.

*   *   *

In another hour, the members of the president's party began drifting into the robing room and the adjacent lounge. I mingled with them, making small talk. Then my three charges arrived together.

"Are you conspiring against me?" I asked them.

"We have decided on a joint presidency in alternate years," said one, to general laughter from the others.

"Get me *The Chronicle of Higher Education*—fast," I replied, using one hand as a mock phone to call the premier publication of the academic world.

They laughed and turned to mingle with the crowd.

"Mum's the word about why you're here," I cautioned. "Be vague, please."

They nodded and walked away. Since they would not be marching, they would not be putting on robes.

Soon, a small group of men and one woman wearing civilian clothes and earpieces entered the room. They fanned out around the perimeter. All chatter stopped as those inside turned to face the door.

President Sykes entered first, talking animatedly with a distin-
guished-looking man with the posture and presence of someone
who was used to being in charge and being deferred to.

Paul Bickford followed them in, leaning over to whisper in
the general's ear.

"You may be at ease," said General Chang. Then he laughed
heartily, joined first by the president, then by everyone else in
the room.

We all chatted absent-mindedly about nothing in particular as
people who have never met before often do. We were killing time
while we waited for someone to tell us what to do next. These
were people who were used to being cared for by handlers. It was
not a bad way to get through a busy day. You get a schedule in the
morning and follow it until night. Today, I was one of those handlers, so I kept an eye on my watch to know when to move my
charges out of the Alumni Center and over to the stadium.

As the group talked, several women from the president's
office walked around, adjusting robes and hoods. One replaced
a rather bedraggled-looking hood with a newer one; another
whispered to one of the vice provosts, who soon slipped out of
her wrinkled robe into one that looked newly pressed.

After about a half-hour of chatting and sipping coffee, the
chief marshal stepped to the center of the room.

"Good morning, ladies and gentlemen, President Sykes,
General Chang." He doffed his tricornered cap trimmed in
ermine and bowed slightly. Roger Goldberg had received his
Ph.D. degree abroad, where academic regalia was much more
elaborate than in the U.S. "We are ready to proceed to the stag-
ing area up the hill to the library. That's where the procession
will begin. Please be up there by half past the hour."

Even a dignified crowd in the finest garb can look momentarily confused. The men and women around me seemed

unsure as to what to do next until President Sykes took over by letting out a very unprecedented whistle. "Follow me," he shouted, taking the general's arm and steering him through the door. The agents with the earpieces set up a loose cordon around the two of them. The other members of the soon-to-be procession fell in behind. I let my three candidates have more coffee while I talked to Paul Bickford.

"Looks like you've got things well in hand," I said, as we moved out of earshot of the others.

"It is quiet," he said. "Maybe too quiet. We aren't getting any of the normal Internet chatter or even radio or phone interceptions. Those guys are always threatening to do something. We tend to worry when they go silent, like the proverbial dog that didn't bark in the night."

"Is Chang a particular target?"

"Not the general himself, but the office he holds. Terrorists like to have notches on their *Kalashnikovs*, so to speak. Knock off an important man, and you get bragging rights in the madrasahs in Pakistan. Little boys want to be like you when they grow up."

He glanced at the three people chatting in the corner.

"Your guys will be fine. Just keep an eye out for anything suspicious. I'll have a man outside the door of the box. If you see anything out of the ordinary, tell him, and he'll relay the message to me right away. I wouldn't sweat it. Just remember to be alert to everything that is going on around you."

"Like in the Arctic. You said the same thing then and look what happened," I laughed, but shook my head as I recalled what had happened on the research expedition where Bickford and I had met.

"Yes, I did, but I came through for you at the end, didn't I?"

"You did, indeed. You saved my ass and several other people, too."

"Do you ever see Miss Baugh and Mr. Salcedo?"

Jane Baugh and Bobby Salcedo were the only two members of the ice expedition who survived, along with me. Although we vowed to stay in close touch after our mutual ordeal was over, we had not done so. We lived too far apart for that. And I think we reminded one another of harrowing experiences we'd just as soon forget.

"Not as much as I'd like."

"They are great people. Miss Baugh is an amazing person," said Bickford. "To do all she did at her age—I was in awe. Mr. Salcedo is pretty unconventional, but very skilled at what he does."

I hadn't heard Bickford share a personal observation—or utter a kind word—about anyone before. His nostalgia was surprising and a bit touching. A loner like Bickford probably seldom connected with anyone. I hoped he felt similarly close to me. The moment ended abruptly, though, when one of his men appeared in the doorway.

"Tom, good talking to you." He turned on his heel and was gone within seconds.

I walked over to the three people in my care. "It's time to move along."

*   *   *

We were in our places in the president's box by 1:45 P.M. Mrs. Sykes was as gracious a lady as I had ever met in that difficult position. Women married to university presidents are like the wives of presidents of the United States. They did not seek their unsalaried posts, but were expected to attend hundreds of events throughout the year, always knowing the right thing to say, always able to put people at ease, always able to suffer fools—and we have many fools in the academic world.

"You are very welcome to our humble abode," she said with a hearty laugh as she gestured around the skybox. "I have been entertaining your wives this morning and was pleased to find how much we have in common."

The women who looked to be the same age as Mrs. Sykes walked over to their husbands and hugged and air kissed them. Not too much passion there, I thought to myself. One looked assertive and one a bit mousy. But what did I know? My first impressions of people are usually way off the mark.

Other luminaries who were present resumed talking—a state senator here, a state Supreme Court justice there, a big donor whose child was graduating over in the corner. Invitations to the president's box for commencement were not given out haphazardly.

At precisely 2 P.M., I heard the mournful strains of the bagpipers' dirge wafting through the warm afternoon air. The academic procession was nearing the stadium. We walked down the steps to the rows of seats. Mrs. Sykes pushed the large sliding windows open.

"I'd like to hear the pipers and the speeches," she said, "even though we've got all these TV sets."

We could see the color guard and the dark-robed figures close behind, led by the president and the general. They moved along at a steady pace, in pairs, chatting nonchalantly to one another. I was in awe of being in this ceremony every time I participated. I could act nonchalant as well as the next person, but I was really quite proud to be a part of a place that meant so much to me and to which I had given many years of my professional life.

Behind the double row of special guests and various vice provosts, vice presidents, and deans came the students. In a phalanx of uneven rows like an army, the young people walked in. They were arrayed by college, with faculty marshals keeping them more or less in order. But getting college students to do anything too orderly on this, the biggest day in their lives so far, was hard. Many sauntered, others marched, and half were talking on cell phones, in conversations that probably began with "Guess where I am!"

The crowd let out a murmur of approval and then started applauding, a continuous din that would last much of the afternoon. Everyone in the large crowd had much to applaud about. For many proud parents, commencement meant the end of high tuition bills. For spouses, commencement signified the start of a new, presumably better paid, life. Commencement was a big day for everyone.

In the half-hour it took for the students to walk to their seats in a serpentine pattern that was fascinating to watch, those of us in the skybox continued to chat, eat from an assortment of meat, cheese and desserts, and drink coffee. Although I missed being an active participant in the ceremony, it was fun to view it from this rarefied distance.

Then at 2:30 P.M. the ceremony itself began. I wondered how it felt to the president to be presiding over his last commencement. He had been an average chief executive—a caretaker more than an innovator. How would the new president handle the job? Would the next few years hold more of the same or exciting change?

If those of us on the search committee had a crystal ball, we'd all be better off. But we did not, and thousands of people—both faculty and staff—would be affected by our decision. I hoped it would be the right one.

*   *   *

By 3:45 P.M., the speeches were over and the awarding of diplomas was winding down. I always dreaded the Ph.D. segment for the time it took. Each student—easily several hundred—had his or her name read and was hooded by his or her major professor. This part of commencement harked back to medieval times in its ritualistic effect. I knew from my own experience how much this meant to student and faculty member. It was, after all, the culmination of many years of work. The professor was sending the student out into the world; the hooding marked the transfer of knowledge. It was a magical moment.

Unfortunately it was also a long, drawn-out process that interrupted what the majority of people in attendance had come to witness: the awarding of degrees to over three thousand undergraduates. It was hard to keep a lid on all that testosterone, adolescent energy, and impatience. It was hard to keep the students from talking loudly with their seatmates and on their cell phones. It was hard to keep them in their seats and in the order of rank they would need to maintain to get the diplomas with their names on them as they crossed the stage a bit later.

I had been a marshal before, so I knew the difficulty. Happily, on this day I was not responsible. I could view the semichaotic scene from the distance of the president's box and hope we got to that final part of the program as quickly as possible.

Now, at 3:50 P.M., the deans of the various colleges were giving out the actual leather cases, one a minute, to a steady stream of students. As they had done at Oregon University for years, each student took the case, opened it, and checked the name on the diploma inside. Then they laughed or cried or smiled or pumped the air to the cheers of friends and family in the audience.

Most eyes in the audience were glued to one of two giant television screens sitting on either side of the stage. Their presence and the use of the football stadium as the site for commencement represented the end of an intimacy that had been present in the nearby basketball pavilion. Now the spectators could see the students get their degrees up close, but to me, it seemed that the important transfer had become remote and impersonal.

By 4:15 P.M., half the members of the presidential party were either dozing or in a state that practitioners of meditation call zoning out. I was sitting between two of the candidates, as we listened to the university band play "Pomp and Circumstance," "Londonderry Air," and "Fanfare for the Common Man" for easily the tenth time.

A glint of sunlight caught my eye from across the stadium. No one was supposed to be on that side today because the half-finished structure was still not safe. I dismissed any concerns about trouble when I remembered the extra security precautions for General Chang. Paul Bickford would have that side of the stadium locked down tight. Some security guy's glasses had caused the reflection, I was quite sure.

Seconds later, I saw the tiny pinpoint of light from the scope of a high-powered rifle dart back and forth on the chest of the candidate to my left. Before I could react, I heard a whooshing sound and he slumped in his seat, a small spot of blood beginning to run down the front of his shirt. The candidate on my right took that moment to stand up. As he did, I heard another whooshing sound, and he staggered forward. I reached to grab him, but the momentum of his forward fall caused him to career out of the open window of the skybox. Seconds later, I heard people screaming as his body fell into the wooden seats below, undoubtedly injuring those sitting in them. Amid the scramble of feet and more crying and yelling, I still heard the melancholy music, which now seemed more like a dirge than an upbeat accompaniment to this previously joyous day.

PART TWO

Moving at a Glacial Pace
May 2004 to June 2005

I spotted the woman as soon as she entered the courtroom while I waited to see if I would be picked for jury duty. I had come early to observe some of the proceedings. As she walked up to the wooden railing that separated the spectators from the front half of the courtroom, she paused momentarily before pushing through the gate. The loud clang from its metal hinges competed with the clap of her wedge-style shoes in disturbing the quiet of the courtroom.

With little for us to do while we waited for proceedings to begin, the five of us already there watched the woman. She was short and somewhat stocky, probably in her mid-fifties. Her blonde hair needed retouching, evidenced by the dark roots that were showing. She was wearing a short skirt that was not as sexy as she hoped; instead, it merely emphasized her unattractive legs. They were what my father used to call "piano legs." Her cheap-looking leather coat partially covered a white sleeveless blouse. She was carrying a large backpack and a bottle of Mountain Dew.

Now on the other side of the railing, she did not sit down, but immediately began pacing behind the carved table and four chairs that were grouped there. The judge's bench was on the left, slightly higher than everything else. What I took to be the clerk's desk was on the right, a bit closer to the front, with a computer resting on it. The jury box was on the right wall: two levels, nine chairs, with a railing that separated it from the rest of the courtroom. The witness stand was in the front, flanked by both the American flag and the flag of the State of Oregon. There were two doors in the center of the rear wall. Light came from an old-style gaslight, recessed modern lighting in the high ceiling, and the high curved windows in the left wall—their upper panes of colored glass. The room looked great, its oak furniture and overall appearance very much in keeping with the year the building had been dedicated: 1888. The renovation completed in time for the one-hundredth anniversary of the building had been handled with painstaking precision.

The woman stopped pacing as two other people walked through the swinging gate. An older man in a mismatched plaid suit stepped back to admit a slightly frazzled-looking woman in her forties. She sat down in a chair to the left. He whispered something to the blonde before they both sat down in chairs on the right. Before doing so, however, she took off her coat and laid it and her backpack on one of the chairs lined up along the inside of the railing, I presume for expert witnesses.

As the clock struck nine, the doors at the rear opened. "All rise."

The judge entered at a brisk pace, her black robe rustling faintly in the suddenly hushed room. Her clerk followed closely, saying, "The circuit court is now in session. The Honorable J. Betty Andrews presiding."

The clerk sat behind her desk on a level below the judge and reached over to turn on her computer.

"Please be seated."

The judge looked to be in her forties with a pleasant face and kind eyes.

"We are here in the matter of custody of a minor child, Douglas Acton. The petitioner is the child's mother. Am I correct, Mr. Harcourt?"

The older man on the right rose. "Yes, Your Honor. The child's mother, Angelique Acton-Jones, is here." The blonde woman started to rise, but Harcourt abruptly pushed her back in her seat. The man sat down too, whispering in an agitated way to his client.

"Ms. Brompton, is the state ready to proceed?"

The frazzled-looking woman riffled through a stack of papers in front of her before rising. "Yes, Your Honor." Although her suit appeared expensive, the assistant district attorney already looked a bit disheveled, with the tail of her silk blouse hanging out enough to reveal her bare back. She sat down so quickly that she bounced up slightly from her chair.

"Very well, then," said the judge, "we will proceed. Ms. Brompton."

The assistant D.A. once again riffled through the mound of papers on her desk for a few seconds before finding what she was looking for. She stood up. Then she gulped water from a glass.

"The state will show that Ms. Acton-Jones is not fit to regain custody of her son, a seven-year-old male named . . ." she looked alarmed before finding the name on yet another piece of paper, which she then dropped on the floor. ". . . Douglas Acton."

"You are going to present evidence relating to Ms. Acton-Jones's competence as a parent?"

"Yes, Judge. I have in my hand the report of an incident involving Ms. Acton-Jones, her son, and a male now housed in the Benton County Correctional Facility. He's being held on a charge of child endangerment. He and Ms. . . ."

"His name, Ms. Brompton. Please give us his name for the record."

"Oh, yes. Sorry, Judge." More paper shuffling ensued as the assistant D.A. looked for the magic page. She found what she was looking for and held it high. "Roy Dewayne Richards. Mr. Richards is a convicted pedophile . . ."

"Objection, Your Honor," said Harcourt, the defense attorney. "Mr. Richards is not on trial here and his background is not an issue."

"The court will get to that matter in due time, Mr. Harcourt. Do you have anything more, Ms. Brompton?"

"Nothing at this time, Judge."

"Very well, then, we will proceed. Ms. Acton-Jones, will you please take the stand and be sworn in?"

The blonde got up from her chair, squared her shoulders, and headed for the witness stand, her clunky shoes again making noise on the polished wooden floor. The clerk walked over to stand in front of her; the woman raised her left hand, then her right, then her left again, before the patient clerk whispered to her the proper procedure.

"Under penalty of perjury, do you swear to tell the truth, the whole truth, and nothing but the truth?"

The blonde nodded.

"Please speak up, for the record," said the judge.

"I do," said the blonde.

"Please be seated."

The blonde's shoes made another clomping sound as she arranged herself in the witness chair.

"State your name and place of residence."

"Angelique Lelani Acton-Jones."

She smiled at her attorney and glanced at the judge.

"Place of residence?"

The blonde's face looked blank.

"Where you live?"

"Oh yeah. I see. North Cascades Mobile Home Park, number 103. I'm not sure of the exact address, but it's out on Highway 99W, near the turnoff to that forest place run by the college. I could . . ."

"That will suffice for the record. The clerk will fill it in later. Now then, Ms. Acton-Jones . . ."

"You can call me Angie if you want to, Judge, I mean Your Honor. I don't mind."

The blonde's attorney was shaking his head vigorously.

"Ms. Acton-Jones, you are petitioning this court to regain custody of your son, a minor child named Douglas Acton?"

"Yes, ma'am, I mean, Judge, that is correct. My little Dougie is the dearest thing in the world to me. He's . . ."

At this point, the room filled with the familiar strains of "Yankee Doodle Dandy," coming from her coat across the room. A look of sheer terror came over the blonde's face. The judge sat impassively, waiting for the ringing to cease.

"Please resume your testimony, Ms. Acton-Jones. You were saying?"

"Sorry, Judge, I mean Your Honor. I was saying that my little Dougie means more to me than life itself. I brought him into this world, and I am going to fight for him with the last breath in my body." And then the blonde started to cry.

The judge nodded to her clerk, who walked to the witness, carrying a box of tissues. The blonde grabbed a fistful and dabbed her eyes.

"Sorry, Your Honor. I just can't help . . ."

Yankee Doodle made its presence known again.

"Ms. Acton-Jones! Will you please take care of your cell phone!"

The blonde got up and clomped rapidly to the railing, pausing to glance nervously at her attorney, who seemed to have slouched even lower in his chair. With the phone still ringing, she grabbed her coat and tried desperately to find it. When it was not in the pocket, she ran her fingers up and down the coat; we were in the fifth rendition of the tune when she finally appeared to locate the device. The problem was that the lining of the coat stood between her and the OFF button.

"My lining is torn," shouted the blonde over her shoulder to the judge, whose face was stern and impassive, although I thought I saw a slight smile beginning to form on her mouth.

The blonde then began to punch desperately at the phone, hoping to connect with the correct button. After another agonizing minute or so, she succeeded and the ringing stopped. She threw the coat on the chair and walked more slowly and less confidently back to the witness stand.

"Now, Ms. Acton-Jones, you were saying?"

"Just that I love my little boy and want him with me."

"Mr. Harcourt. Do you have anything to add to what your client has said?"

The attorney rose slowly, some papers in his hand. "May I approach?"

The judge nodded.

"I have a record of Ms. Acton-Jones's successful treatment in the Lynn-Benton drug rehabilitation program." Harcourt handed the papers to both the judge and the clerk, before returning to his place at the table. "I think this speaks for itself as to Ms. Acton-Jones's desire to turn her life around and return to her proper role as a loving mother." He sat down and gave his client a fatherly pat on the arm.

"Now, Ms. Brompton. As to the matter of Mr. Richards. The question still to be answered is regarding his presence in the house with a minor child."

The assistant D.A. got to her feet and nodded vigorously. Then she drank more water. "Yes, Your Honor. He is a convicted pedophile, and he was living in the same house with Ms. Acton-Jones and the minor child, Daniel Acton."

"I believe his name is Douglas Acton," said the judge.

"Yes, of course. Sorry, Judge."

"Mr. Harcourt, is Mr. Richards now living with Ms. Acton-Jones?"

The attorney leaned over to his client, who whispered in his ear and gestured with both hands. "Yes, Your Honor, it appears that he was before his incarceration."

"In that case, I think we need Mr. Richards in this courtroom before we can proceed. I may need to question him. Bailiff, can the prisoner be produced?"

The judge looked at a fireplug of a man, fairly short and well-built, his shaved head glistening in the lights.

"I can call over there, Your Honor. They are all in the exercise yard now. It might take an hour to transfer him."

"Before I order that, tell us about the incident in question, Ms. Brompton."

The frazzled assistant D.A. once again riffled through a stack of papers before standing. This time, she paused to tuck her blouse back into her skirt.

"On the early evening of August 25, Corvallis police responded to a complaint phoned in to 9-1-1 about a man and a woman fighting in front of a trailer at the North Cascade Mobile Home Park at 6832 North West Highway 99W in Corvallis. Upon arrival, the two officers reported a man brandishing a knife at a woman." She paused to look at Angelique

Acton-Jones, who stared stoically at the flags in the front of the courtroom. "The officers quickly subdued the man—Roy Dewayne Richards—and noticed at that time the presence of a young boy standing behind the woman—Angelique Acton-Jones. He seemed to be crying."

"I was protecting my baby," shouted the blonde from her seat.

"Mr. Harcourt, please control your client."

The attorney again whispered in the blonde's ear.

"I want to talk to Mr. Richards," said the judge. "If we can't get him over here, I'll have to reschedule this hearing until he is in my court. What are we looking at, Margaret?"

She turned to her clerk, who looked at her computer screen and punched a few keys.

"A week from Friday is your first opening."

"That's what we'll do. Ms. Brompton, Mr. Harcourt. We will reconvene to hear from Mr. Richards. Until then, we are adjourned."

"All rise."

The judge picked up the folders in front of her and walked through the door, trailed by her clerk. The blonde looked angry and started gesturing as she whispered none too softly into the ear of her attorney.

"What am I supposed to do in the meantime?" she said. "What about my little boy? He really needs his mommy!"

"You should have thought about that before you got yourself into this mess with your boyfriend!"

"But I love him, and he loves me."

"A convicted pedophile living under the same roof as a seven-year-old boy! You've got to be kidding me if you think this will be easy."

I must have been sitting in just the right place for the sound of their voices to resonate as clearly as if I had been sitting next to them. I glanced at Ms. Brompton, the harried assistant D.A. She seemed not to be listening, but was, instead, attempting to organize her mountain of papers. As she tried to arrange a particularly large pile of them, they suddenly fell onto the floor, flying in every direction. I jumped to my feet to help gather those that had scattered under the railing into the spectator area.

"Here, let me help," I said, gallantly.

"Oh, sure, great, thanks."

She grabbed them from my hand and stuffed everything into an open briefcase. She practically ran from the courtroom, teetering unsteadily on her high heels, shirttail untucked again.

I sat down in the back at the end of a bench—a good observation spot. What I had come for—jury selection—would begin in a half-hour. My potential fellow members of the jury pool were gathering.

The diversity of Corvallis as a town—located in an agricultural valley surrounded by a timber-covered mountain range, with a large university and a large high-tech manufacturer—would probably be reflected in the jury pool.

Sitting around me were a few younger people, a lot of people who looked like retirees, and a smattering of men in suits and ties. I only recognized one face. I did not know Duncan Delgado personally, but I had seen him on campus and read about him in the newspaper.

He was a biologist who did research on viruses and plagues. He was also a political activist, speaking out on a number of causes, including the plight of Vietnam veterans. There was rarely a peace march in Portland where he was not photographed in the front rank of protesters. As a tenured full professor who brought a lot of grant money into the university's coffers, he could get away with his high-profile activities, as long as he did not cross a certain invisible line.

Delgado was probably in his fifties, but looked ten years younger. He was tall and well-built, his dark features accentuated by a huge mane of brown hair flecked with gray. I was surprised when he sat down next to me.

"Can you believe all these yokels," he whispered. "They don't look like they've got the brainpower to carry on a decent conversation, let alone render a verdict."

"I don't believe we've met," I said. "Tom Martindale."

We shook hands.

"Yeah. I know who you are. It'll be good to have someone . . ." he glanced behind us, ". . . intelligent to talk to."

"I don't know much about the case," I said, deciding not to say anything to alienate people I might be spending a lot of time with in the near future.

"A dumb wetback who got his dick in a ringer by killing the owner of a jewelry store he tried to rob," he said. "Pretty much of a slam dunk, if you ask me." He paused to look at me closely. "You surprised I say that about my own people? Shit. I come from a background poorer than his. I made something of myself. He could have too, if he hadn't taken what for him was the easy way. Rob a store." He shook his head. "How dumb is that? A stupid beaner. Shit. A slam dunk."

"Have you ever been on jury duty before, Delgado?"

"Naw. I always got out of it. This case intrigued me a bit, though, I got to admit. I'm Mexican too, so I thought I'd better make sure justice was served." Then he winked at me, instantly negating the worth of the words he had just uttered. "You?"

"My first, too. The journalist in me likes to get the inside track on things. We like to be in the know. I have to admit that I hoped I'd be put on this jury ever since I got my original summons."

"Oh, so you were a reporter before you started teaching? I'd better watch what I say."

Our mundane conversation was interrupted by the entrance of the judge and her clerk.

"All rise. The circuit court is now in session. Judge J. Betty Andrews presiding."

"Please be seated. Good morning, ladies and gentlemen."

There were murmurs of the same salutation to her.

"We are here to select the jury for the trial of Hector Morales, who is charged with homicide in the first-degree in the death of Saul Ivenski. Bailiff, please bring in the prisoner."

At that, the rear door of the courtroom opened and a short man entered, flanked by two sheriff's deputies. He shuffled slowly down the aisle, the shackles binding his hands and ankles clanking loudly with each step. Morales scanned the courtroom as he proceeded to his seat, pausing to look twice at Delgado. His head was shaved. A tattoo of a dragon was visible on his neck, just above the top of his sweatshirt, which had the letters BCCF on the back. A practiced hand at courtroom appearances, he turned around with his back to the deputy who unlocked and removed his handcuffs; the shackles on his ankles remained in place, however.

As this was going on, a youngish-looking Spanish woman with thick brown hair stood up and approached an impeccably dressed man who wore his black hair in a ponytail. I figured he was Morales's attorney.

After the two conferred for several minutes, the attorney spoke quietly to his client, who shook his head slightly. The woman resumed her seat.

"Good morning again, ladies and gentlemen," said the judge. "Are we ready to proceed with jury selection?

Attorneys on both sides stood. The deputy district attorney was the opposite of Morales's lawyer in both looks and attire.

He wore a shapeless brown jacket and baggy khaki pants. His rounded face sported a goatee and mustache.

"My clerk will read some numbers. If your number is called, please sit in the jury box. If your number is not called, you should wait in the hall."

The clerk started calling numbers and in response, people got up and walked through the gate and took seats in the jury box. My number was called right after Delgado's. We sat next to one another in the second row.

"Thank you, Margaret. And thanks to all of you," said the judge, as she looked out at the people sitting in the spectator area. "Please wait in the hall for the time being while we proceed with jury selection."

About ten people got up and walked out of the courtroom.

"Ladies and gentlemen, we are about to proceed with the *voir dire*, the preliminary part of a trial where attorneys for the state and defense ask you questions to determine your background and impartiality as jurors in this trial. You will be sworn in, stating that you are telling the truth, before you answer the questions. If either of these two fine attorneys challenges you—our word for objects to you — as a juror, please do not take it personally. Mr. Bates, please begin."

The rumpled assistant D.A. sprang to his feet and walked to a point directly in front of the jury box. He read from a list of names he held in his hands.

"Mrs. Haggerty."

"Yes," replied the short woman in a pink pantsuit who sat in front of me. Her tightly permed hair had a faint blue tint to it.

"Please tell us what you do."

"I am a homemaker."

"Your husband is still living?"

"Yes, sir. My Pat's in good health."

"Children?"

"Three kids and twelve grandchildren."

"It seems that everyone is in fine fettle in your family."

The others tittered and Mrs. Haggerty blushed.

"Mr. Bates. I don't think we need your misplaced humor. We are not here to comment on the size of our juror's families."

"No, Judge. Sorry." The assistant D.A. continued with his questioning. "Have you ever seen the defendant before? I mean, Mr. Hector Morales over there?" Bates had started a nervous pace back and forth in front of us. When he did stop walking, he arched his feet so that he rocked up and down.

"No, sir. Never in my life."

"No objection to Mrs. Haggerty, Your Honor."

"Mr. Madrid."

The immaculately dressed defense attorney stood in stark contrast to the D.A.; every hair on his head was in place and his unlined face virtually glowed, probably the result of regular visits to a spa. His suit could easily have cost more than I paid for my entire wardrobe.

"Mrs. Haggerty, do you consider yourself a fair person?"

The lady looked confused, as if she had never been asked such a question before. "I guess so."

"I am afraid that guessing is not allowed when it comes to deciding whether a man is guilty of murder."

When Mrs. Haggerty did not answer, Madrid began tapping his pencil on the edge of the table. The judge intervened.

"Mrs. Haggerty, what Mr. Madrid is asking is if you can be fair in deciding Mr. Morales's guilt or innocence."

"You mean whether I'll hold it against him because he's a spic?" Mrs. Haggerty said without a trace of embarrassment.

"The defense challenges this juror, Your Honor."

"You may step down, Mrs. Haggerty. You are excused for the day."

The lady still looked confused, but quickly complied with the judge's directions. She picked up her purse, and was gone from the courtroom within seconds.

"Duncan Delgado," the assistant D.A. read from the list.

The man nudged me in the ribs, rose to his feet, then sat down again. I could tell that he liked to be looked at and admired. He was good looking, but it seemed to me that he probably used his good looks to get what he wanted from others, that he hoped the people he encountered in life would be so in awe of him that he could get whatever he wanted from them. It was an arrogant view of the world, but I suspected that it was probably true of him.

As Bates approached the jury box and the resplendent Delgado, the difference between the two men became even more apparent.

"What do you do, Mr. Delgado?"

"It's *Doctor* Delgado, actually, Mr. Bates. I have a Ph.D."

"Sorry. *Doctor* Delgado."

"I am a tenured professor of biology at Oregon University, specializing in the study of viruses. I have a large number of ongoing research projects, most of them funded by the United States government." Delgado smiled as if to savor his standing in society.

"The state has no problem with this juror. I accept him."

Madrid stood up and approached the jury box.

"You are obviously of Hispanic ancestry, Dr. Delgado," he said. "Do you think you can be fair in rendering a verdict in this case? I mean, you might be just the opposite of our previous juror candidate, the unfortunate Mrs. Haggerty."

"I'll ask that you not refer to Mrs. Haggerty in that way, or at all," said the judge. "She is not connected in any way to the matters before us."

"You are right, Judge Andrews. I am sorry. Can you be fair, Dr. Delgado?"

"Yes, sir, I can," said Delgado, suddenly becoming humble before our eyes. He betrayed none of the prejudice he had displayed earlier, when he told me that he wanted to be on the jury.

"The defense accepts the juror," said Madrid, sitting down.

Both sides questioned, then accepted the next six jurors quickly. They were evenly divided between men and women, with four whites, one Black, and one Hispanic. Their ages ranged from early twenties to sixty, in my casual calculation. Then it was my turn.

"Thomas Martindale."

I held up my hand.

Bates walked to the jury box briskly.

"Tell us what you do, sir."

"I am a journalism professor at Oregon University."

"How long have you been at the university, Mr. Martindale?"

"Over fifteen years."

"Do you know the defendant, Mr. Hector Morales?"

Both Morales and Madrid turned to look at me, as if they were trying to decide if they knew me.

"No, I have never seen him before."

"I have no problem with this juror, Your Honor. The state accepts Mr. Martindale."

For me, Madrid decided he needed a closer look and walked over to stand at the end of the jury box next to where I was sitting in the second row.

"It says on your juror questionnaire that you were once an investigative reporter for a magazine in New York."

"Yes, that's right. For eight years."

"Did you cover crime in that job?"

"On occasion, yes. But a lot of other subjects as well—politics, the environment . . ."

"Just answer the question, Mr. Martindale."

I could feel my face become red as it always did when I was embarrassed. "Sorry."

"What about race and nationality?"

"The civil rights problems in the South on occasion."

"Problems of illegal immigration along the border?"

"No, I never did any stories there."

Madrid paused and rubbed his temples, as if he was trying to remember something he obviously already was prepared to talk about.

"Haven't I read about you in the papers, Mr. Martindale?"

"I'm not sure what you're talking about. There have been stories about me when I've been promoted or written a book or article, I guess."

"Isn't it true, Mr. Martindale . . ." He paused for some kind of dramatic effect. "You are *Mister*, is that right, or should it be *Doctor?*"

"No, Mister is correct. I don't have a Ph.D."

Why was he making such a big thing out of my title? Was he somehow comparing me with Delgado? If so, I couldn't figure out why.

"Have you not been involved in several well-publicized cases where you helped the police solve crimes and catch the bad guys?"

"I'm not sure how well-publicized they were but, yes, I guess you could say that."

"And I think the last one resulted in the death of one of your students, a young woman."

Why was Madrid making it sound like the wrong people had been arrested and tried for those crimes, and that I had been the obvious culprit?

"My involvement, as you put it, had nothing to do with the death of the student. I just helped determine the person who killed her."

"So, you like this amateur sleuth work, do you, Mr. Martindale?"

"I wouldn't call it that. I guess I enjoy figuring things out. Being a reporter is sometimes like solving a puzzle."

"Would you be inclined to do a bit of investigating of your own in this case, Mr. Martindale? I mean, to help the police with their work?"

Angela Pride often accuses me of just that, but I wasn't about to admit it here. Besides, I preferred to think of it as helping friends in trouble.

"No, Mr. Madrid, that would not be my role."

"I wonder." The attorney rubbed his temples again for guidance before speaking. "The defense challenges this juror."

"Thank you, Mr. Martindale. You are dismissed with the thanks of the court."

As I got up from my chair, Delgado patted my knee.

"Too bad, old man," he sneered. "I guess your past caught up with you."

I walked through the swinging gate, out the door of the courtroom, down the hall, down the main stairway, and was back on Fourth Street within minutes. My career as a juror was over as quickly as it began.

It didn't take a Ph.D. to figure out why Madrid had challenged me, I thought as I drove up to campus. He decided I'd do too much second-guessing. Maybe he didn't like the press either. In Delgado, however, he felt he had someone who would be sympathetic to his client, a fellow Hispanic who had risen from humble beginnings and would want to give Hector Morales the chance to do that too. He didn't know that Delgado was more prejudiced than I could ever be.

I was sorry to not be part of what looked like an interesting case. Reporters—and journalism professors who used to be reporters—are always voyeurs when it comes to examining the underside of life.

But I sloughed all of this off as I parked my car and walked to my office. The campus was beautiful on this spring afternoon. The trees and bushes that lined the walks and surrounded the buildings were brimming with new leaves and blossoms. We have a lot of rain in Oregon, but it shows its beneficial results in the profusion of green.

My phone was ringing as I unlocked the door to my outer office. I got to it on the third ring. "Hello."

"Tom. It's Hadley Collins."

"Hi, Hadley. How are you?"

"Good, Tom, but too busy, as always. I wanted to tell you that I've recommended you for a new committee."

Hadley Collins was the vice president for university relations, which means that she oversaw communications and public relations. Two years ago, I had worked for her by acting as the liaison between the university and a Portland production house to prepare some television commercials. Madrid had referred to this earlier in the day in talking about my crime solving. The student who was killed had been in the journalism department, and I had helped clear the kid accused of her murder.

"Not the image enhancement committee," I groaned. "I'm not sure I can take all those people again."

"No, nothing like that," said Hadley, chuckling as she recalled the memory of endless wrangling and constant pontificating by a few of the members. "I'd rather not talk about this over the phone. Are you free right now? Can you come down?"

"I've got nothing all the rest of the day. I'd cleared my schedule because I thought I'd be serving on a jury, but I got bumped so here I am. I'll be there in ten minutes."

✳   ✳   ✳

Like those of most other vice presidents, Hadley Collins's office was on the sixth floor of the administration building. In contrast to much of the rest of campus, the sixth floor was always quiet, like a church or a library. Everyone talked in hushed tones, their shoes not making any sounds on the thick carpets.

"Hi, Nancy. Great to see you," I said to her friendly assistant, who I had known for years. In fact, Nancy Plumb had even been my secretary many years ago.

"My God, call Security. We restrict access to people like you."

I reached over and hugged her. "Why do I think you really mean that?"

"Vice President Collins is expecting you. Go on in."

"I'll see you later, Nancy." I pointed a finger at her and made a makeshift gun by bringing my thumb down to it.

"Knock, knock," I said to Hadley, who had her back to me as she sat in front of her computer. At the sound of my voice, she turned around, a big smile on her face.

"Hi, Tom. Come in and sit down. Would you like coffee?"

"Yeah, I'd love some."

Hadley walked to the door. "Nancy, two cups of your finest blend. Black for Tom." Sitting back down, she asked, "Things going well for you, Tom?"

"Not bad. I like my classes but wish I could cut back on my committee stuff so I could do more writing."

Nancy bustled into the room and put down the cups of coffee, carefully placing coasters under them. "Watch this guy, Vice President Collins." She patted my shoulder as she walked out the door and closed it.

"I wanted to talk to you about a new committee assignment, one that could be the most important of your time here," Hadley continued. She paused for effect and sipped some coffee.

"You wanted my attention?" I laughed. "You've got it!"

"As you know, President Sykes is retiring at the end of the year. You also know that a search committee will be recommending candidates to replace him. I have been given the task of setting up the committee. I will also be its vice-chair. Dimitri

Chekhov, a physics professor, will be chair. I'd like you to be a member and also secretary. I don't mean that you'd be taking minutes or anything mundane like that. I mean you'd be the person who keeps track of the paper flow and supervises arrangements when the final candidates come to campus."

We both drank more coffee.

"It isn't like you to be so quiet, Tom. Are you going to turn me down?"

"On the contrary, Hadley. I'd love to do this. It would be an honor and a challenge. Count me in."

"Good, I'm glad to hear it. I was impressed with your work in coordinating the advertising campaign. You didn't ever let all the unpleasantness get in the way of our goals. The ads got done, and now our enrollment is up—the ads played an important role in that."

"I should have asked for a dollar for every new student."

We both laughed. "We will staff the search out of this office. In fact, I can even offer you office space on the other side of the building, right here on this floor. It will come in handy when the search really gets rolling. You can store all the materials there. I also intend to ask your chairman to give you one less course for the next fall and winter terms."

"What more can I ask," I said. "Seems like you've thought of everything."

"I'm glad you're pleased."

"Who are the other members of the committee?"

"You're only the second person I've asked, after Dimitri. Here's the tentative list."

She handed me a single sheet of paper. I scanned the list and saw that I knew—or knew of—everyone on it. Besides Hadley, Dimitri, and me, there were Liz Stein, a political science professor; Chad Nunn, an oceanographer; Miguel Gomez, head of the Hispanic Studies program; Gloria Gordon, the former president of the Alumni Association; Alex Crandell, a member of the State Board of Education; Victoria Chen, a senior in chemical engineering; and Ricky Lee Washington, a junior in liberal studies.

"These look like good choices," I said, handing the page back to her. "Very diverse."

"Thanks. Keep the list. I talked to a number of people as I decided on the final choices. It's probably the most important committee any of us has ever been on. I know you feel that a lot of committee work is superfluous, Tom, but this isn't one of them. It's really important."

"I know it is. I will take it as seriously as I've ever taken any campus assignment."

"Any questions?"

"Only one. What's the timeline for getting a new person into the job?"

"It's May now, so we hope to have someone in place by a year from August," said Hadley.

"Like everything else in academe, this will take a lot more time than it would outside, in the real world," I said.

"I wish I could say it would result in a better outcome," she said, shaking her head. "I guess we do belabor things a bit too much, but that's the way we do things and we're stuck with it. Let me show you your office."

We got up and walked down the hall to a smaller warren of offices on the back side of the building.

"This is it, your home sweet home," she smiled, stepping aside to let me enter what looked like a ten-by-ten-foot space containing a desk, a chair, two filing cabinets, and two visitor chairs. The one window overlooked the roofs of the shop and maintenance buildings below.

"Here are your keys. One is for this office, the other is for the building, in case you need to work late." She smiled, knowing I would be doing a lot of that, by choice and by necessity. "And here is your after-hours building pass, in case anyone challenges your presence here on a Saturday night."

"How well you know me," I said. "One workaholic to the other. You set it all up so well. What if I'd turned you down?"

"I know you a lot better than you think I do," she winked. "I'll let you settle in. Just ask Nancy if you need anything. You might start thinking about the selection process."

I walked over and sat behind the desk, then opened all the drawers in turn, to see if the previous occupant had left anything interesting behind. All I uncovered was a few stray paper clips, a box of rubber bands, and some ballpoint pens that had long since run out of ink.

What I found in the IN box interested me the most: the ever-thorough Hadley Collins had compiled a stack of material about presidential searches. I grabbed a yellow legal pad and a new ballpoint pen stored in the OUT box and started taking notes from an article in a publication for people in higher education.

Over 300 colleges and universities choose presidents each year. *Oregon University not alone,* I scribbled. *Might narrow pool of applicants?*

The process is often imperfect because it is a function of people, their strengths and weaknesses, and schedules. *Could be logistical nightmare?* I wrote. *Just like setting up and attending any committee meeting.*

Consultants shape the process and this usually results in a candidate from traditional academic backgrounds. *What about someone from left field—nonacademic—to shake up place?* I noted.

Although consultants aim to identify people who are able to handle the job, the "chemistry" between the candidates and committee members is often the deciding factor in who gets the job. *Getting the right "fit" triumphs,* I wrote. *Pig in a poke?*

Participation by faculty, staff, alumni, students, and interested outside parties can be unwieldy, but often pays off because of the diversity of viewpoints. *All axes get ground,* I scribbled. *If everyone gets fair hearing, all share in the first success.*

The search needs to be thorough, with extensive interviews of not only the candidates, but also their family, friends, faculty, and students at their current institution, the financial condition of that institution, business leaders and media people in that town, even next-door neighbors. *Same thoroughness if person from outside ivy-covered walls,* I noted. *Leave no skeleton unearthed.*

Search committees often go into the process wanting everything under the sun in a new leader, but see the need for compromise when faced with real people and their strengths and weaknesses. *Nobody's perfect,* I penned. *What if no one measures up? Time not on our side.*

Next, I looked at the report written by the last person to have the job I was taking on. Before Art Long left the university for a job at another college, he had prepared a useful report addressed "To my successor as search coordinator:"

> *I went into the job without knowing much about what to do. I had to learn fast. Because the president did not give us as much notice as was usually the case, I had five months when it usually takes one year.*
>
> *Although a presidential search is officially started by the State Board of Education, after they get things rolling, they turn it all over to us. We pay for it.*
>
> *The first thing to do is write a position description and get the committee to agree on it—not always an easy task. Next*

came advertising in local, state, and national publications. *(See attached list, plus contact information.)*

I would suggest that you change the locks on the door of your office for security reasons. I don't think it is paranoid to be concerned about security—nosy people from campus and outsiders with a vested interest in knowing who has applied could be lurking around.

And then there is the media. While the public—especially the many campus "publics"—has a right to know what the committee is doing, you don't want information to get out prematurely. You need to do your research on the candidates and not let reporters do it for you, especially by turning up embarrassing stuff. You need to find this out before anyone else does. I followed the wise advice from a dean I used to work for: don't have any surprises.

But the media will be pounding on your door. Once it is known that you are coordinating the search, you need to figure out what you can and cannot say. For the first couple months, all I ever said was, "The committee is on track. We have a good pool of candidates."

I spent the first month organizing files. I color coded every file folder and gave it a number. When a dossier was ready, I had everything copied; I kept track of the files and had members check them out like books from a library. I stressed the need for confidentiality with all members.

After the deadline for applications, I went through the stack to eliminate people who did not qualify. You know, there are people who apply for every job opening, regardless of their qualifications.

With this out of the way, I turned over the files of the people remaining to subgroups of the committee for further sorting. Out of all this you hope to come up with a pool of *twenty-five people. These are the ones you want to have the committee interview. I could call them the semifinalists and you should hope to have them selected in about three months, given everyone's busy schedule and the hard job of setting up meetings. Someone in higher authority than you needs to stress to the members of the committee how vital their task is. They need to put almost everything but maybe their teaching on hold and concentrate on this assignment. If they can't, they should not agree to serve.*

Once you've narrowed things down to the semifinalists, teams of your members need to fan out across the country to interview them. I'd pick hotels near airports in all parts of the country—like Chicago, Denver, Los Angeles, Atlanta, Washington, New York. The cities will depend on where your people come from. You going to them saves time and money.

After these interviews, pick ten or twelve finalists. You must bring them to hotels in Portland for interviews; I would not bring them to campus. All committee members should attend these sessions. It is crucial to narrow your number to five or six people now. You need to control all of this; if you are not a detail person, you won't survive in the job. You need to be one step ahead of everyone else and not be blind-sided by anyone on the inside or outside.

A final word about budget: I'd aim for $50,000. You won't get it, but it's a good goal. I wish you good luck and good hunting.

— Arthur J. Long

I put the report back into its folder. Art had done a great job. I would be pleased to be half as efficient as he had been.

I was startled by the buzz of the phone on the desk. Hadley Collins had already gotten me listed.

"Tom Martindale."

"Hi, Tom. It's Noreen in the journalism department."

"Hello. How's my favorite secretary?"

"Looking forward to the weekend, if you want to know the truth. Tom, there is a woman here who says she has a 4 P.M. appointment with you. A Maxine March." Her voice dropped to a whisper. "Kind of attractive for an older woman—like you, Tom."

"Quit smirking, Noreen. By the way, I'm not an older woman."

"You know what I mean, Tom."

I was glancing at my trusty date book as I sparred with her. There at four was my penciled entry. *"M. March. To discuss graduate work in department."*

"God, Noreen. I got so involved in all this search stuff, I completely forgot. Tell her I'm on my way. I'll be there in ten minutes!"

Maxine March was standing a bit down the hall from my office reading the items on a bulletin board. I always wonder if people pretend to read bulletin boards as a way to blend into their surroundings. In this case, she can't have cared about what she saw there—the board belonged to the next department in our building: soil science.

"Hi. Ms. March? I'm Tom Martindale."

Up close, Maxine March was very pretty. I could see that as soon as she smiled and focused her big blue eyes on me. She was tall and had a great figure, even in the baggy outfit many students wore. Even though her outfit had probably come from Abercrombie & Fitch, it gave her a slightly revolutionary look.

As she walked into my office, she took off her beret, allowing her long chestnut-colored hair to fall to her waist. I recalled a scene from an old movie I once saw where the librarian unpins her hair from a topknot and removes her glasses. Whereupon the hero says something like, "Miss Jones, you're beautiful!"

"Let's sit out here," I said, indicating my outer office and pulling out a chair from a table I use for small seminars and committee meetings. I ducked into my office at the rear and put my committee materials on my desk, then grabbed a graduate brochure and returned to sit across from Ms. March.

"So, what did you have in mind?"

"I'm new to the area and don't know many people. I thought it would be nice to take some classes and even get a graduate degree."

"Okay." I hesitated while I found the proper section of the brochure and handed it to her. "This spells out what we've got. We don't actually offer a straight graduate degree in journalism."

"As opposed to a crooked one?" She smiled. She had my kind of slightly off-the-wall humor. I like that, and I was beginning to like her.

"You might say that if you were a wise-ass." I was frowning. By this time, she was, too.

"I'm sorry. I was just kidding."

I smiled. "So was I. Just testing your ability to think under fire."

She relaxed again. "You had me worried for a minute."

I waved away her concerns.

"As I was saying, our degree has one of those academic buzzwords connected to it: interdisciplinary. That means the courses that make up your degree will come from several departments. Journalism can be one of them, but there must be two others."

"I see. Okay. But I can concentrate my courses here?"

"Oh, yes. Absolutely. What's your undergraduate degree in?"

"English Lit. A great way to read a lot of good books and discuss them, but the degree doesn't lead to anything you can make a living at doing."

"Yeah, I guess you're right. It's an old argument around here. Knowledge for knowledge's sake or training you can use to get a job. Literature people really look down their noses at us journalism types. Actually, students need lots of everything. Did you plan on a career in journalism?"

She reached down and pulled out a camera from the large bag she had placed next to her chair.

"I hope to make this my source of livelihood." She placed an older-model Leica camera in front of me. I picked it up.

"Very nice."

Even in this age of digital cameras, it was hard to match the quality of a 35 mm Leica—it had been capturing images for some of the world's finest photographers since its invention in 1924.

"It's my pride and joy. It's about the only thing of value my former husband didn't take from me." She was frowning again.

"Sorry."

How could any man treat this lovely woman that shabbily, to leave her with nothing more than a Leica and pseudo-camo clothes? I wanted to find out more, but decided against it.

"Did you plan to start classes in the fall?"

"I hope to take a few this summer, actually."

"I'm afraid we aren't offering much this summer. Did you take the Graduate Record Exam?"

She pulled out a postcard from her bag and handed it to me.

"Wow. Great scores."

"Thanks. I've always done well on tests."

"I'm just the opposite—I usually screw them up. I absolutely hate tests. Okay then. So, what did you have in mind to take for starters?"

"What are you teaching?"

"Nothing too interesting until next spring term. I'm involved in a big project, so I won't have time to teach. Then I'll be doing a course in magazine writing."

"Maybe I can take that one. But I'd like to start sooner—like this fall."

I got up and grabbed a fall term printout from a file drawer, catching a whiff of exotic perfume as I walked past her.

"Photography courses, media law, public affairs reporting, copyediting."

"Maybe a photo course of some kind?" she said.

"I gather you know how to take photos, or you wouldn't have a Leica."

She held the camera close as if to guard it. "I got this from my dad as a birthday gift before he died. He was a crime photographer in the fifties in Chicago. He said he wanted me to have the best camera money could buy. I've been taking photos ever since. I sold some even. I worked at a few alternative weeklies in Chicago and later in Berkeley. Lots of antiwar stuff. Vietnam and all that."

"You don't look old enough to have been involved in all that craziness."

Her eyes flashed. "It was not craziness to those of us in the movement. It was very important, and it helped end the war— I really believe that."

"I didn't mean that . . ."

"The 'craziness' came from the establishment in those days, people in authority. Johnson, then Nixon, and the 1968 Democratic convention in Chicago. We got our skulls cracked night after night."

"You were at the 1968 Democratic Party convention in Chicago? You were one of the protesters there?"

"Yes, I was, and I am proud of it!" Her eyes flashed again, as if daring me to argue with her. I put up both hands to ward off any negative thoughts of me.

"I think you should be proud of anything you did there. I was a journalist then, but I was working in New York and didn't get to Chicago. I was sickened when I saw what the Chicago police did to all of you. How'd you get involved?"

She relaxed a bit and smiled at the memory. "I was a student at the University of Illinois Circle Campus and started going to protest meetings. As the convention got closer, outside people came in to pull the rabble into something cohesive. Everything was orchestrated for maximum exposure on television. The whole world was watching, just like the street chant said."

She paused and looked at me again, a sadness in her eyes.

"In some respects, we were used. Those outsiders didn't get hit over the head and arrested. They were watching from the sidelines, calling the next moves from their megaphones. I got seduced figuratively—the thrill of protesting something big, I guess. And then I got seduced literally—love, sex, and rock-'n'roll. I met my future husband there. Duncan was the most charismatic guy I'd ever met. And he was beyond good looking." She smiled again at the memory.

"What happened to Duncan?"

"Oh, he teaches here at the university. Duncan Delgado is a professor in biology. He's kind of famous. I guess that's why he divorced me, so he could be free to fuck all those pretty young lab assistants."

Before I could reply, she stood up, said she'd be in touch, and walked out the door.

I thought about Maxine March on and off for the rest of the day. As I conducted my classes and then graded papers later, her beautiful face kept intruding.

Duncan Delgado also intrigued me, both as her former husband and as someone involved in the antiwar movement. I was sure that kind of activity had surfaced in the search process when he got his job. Then again, maybe it hadn't. I knew of an assistant football coach whose somewhat shady past had been ignored by search committee members who were more interested in a winning team.

That night, I went to the Google search engine and typed in his name. Within seconds, the first of twenty-five screens of data blinked back at me from the screen. Most dealt with his academic work as a biologist and consisted of references to various papers he had written for academic journals and conferences he had attended as a member of a panel or keynote speaker. There was a smattering of awards as well, including one as Hispanic Scientist of the Year.

While not a candidate for a Nobel Prize or a member of the National Academy of Science, Duncan Delgado had done very well.

I found very little biographical data, beyond a sketchy paragraph that accompanied one of his articles: Ph.D. from UCLA, faculty positions at the University of Maryland and the University of New Mexico; work as a consultant to the Department of Defense; and U.S. Army officer.

It was all pretty vague, and the reporter and voyeur in me wanted to know more. I reached for the phone and dialed a number I hadn't called in a long time. It was answered after one ring.

"Do you have any idea what time it is, Martindale?" The voice was neither nasty nor enthusiastic. Paul Bickford seldom allowed himself to express any emotion.

"It's only eleven, Paul. I knew you'd be awake."

At one point in our time together in the Arctic the year before, Bickford had given me his card. I had tucked it away, thinking I would never use it.

"Long time, no see," I said. "How'd you get away from those Russians I last saw you with?"

"If I told you, I'd have to kill you." His standard line, said in a voice that was flat and determined. While most people used that phrase to get a laugh, Bickford probably meant it. "Whaddya need, Tom?"

"Okay, Paul. No small talk. I want you to get some background information on a guy here at the university."

"You have a legitimate reason to want to know more about this guy? Or are you screwing his wife or something?"

I felt my face turn red as it always did when someone got embarrassingly close to my private thoughts.

"I'm on a search committee here on campus for a new university president. I'm in charge of researching the candidates.

This guy's name came up, and he's got some military connections. I figured you'd be the guy to dig up some stuff on him."

I occasionally lie outright to get what I want. Hell, maybe Delgado would wind up as part of the search. And maybe Bickford could help me get information on some of the real candidates. I'd leave that door open with Bickford, if he helped me now.

The line was completely silent as I waited him out. I had learned long ago that it did not help to chatter away to fill the silence when dealing with someone like Paul Bickford. You only wound up feeling stupid.

"What makes you think I have access to any information that you couldn't get? Ever hear of using a search engine on the Internet?"

"I did that and got very little. I won't dignify the first part of your question with an answer—we both know that you are far more than the private security consultant that you claim to be. You've got more connections than the average guy. I mean, we all knew on the voyage that you were Army Special . . ."

"Not over the phone, Tom. Shut up about that kind of thing! When we worked together last year, you didn't strike me as a blabbermouth. Now, what's this guy's name?"

"Duncan Delgado."

"I'll see what I can do."

"Thanks, Paul. I appreciate it. If this works out, will you help me with other people?"

"I can't promise. Let's see how this works out. Nice to hear from you, Tom. I enjoyed our conversations on the ship."

"Me too, Paul. It will be fun to work with you again."

It was amazing for Bickford to show any sign of friendship. To me, he had always seemed the classic loner. Our "conversations," as he called them, were not long exchanges on the issues of the day or even the weather. Instead, it was more like, "Watch your back, Martindale," or "I'm sorry, but I can't tell you any more"—and sometimes without the "sorry."

"You'll be hearing from me. Give me your phone number and e-mail address."

I rattled off both.

"This is between us, Tom—you and me. And whatever I dig up, it didn't come from me. By the way, I'm back in uniform now."

Before I could reply to that, the line went dead. Stealthful as always, Bickford was gone.

After dinner, I went back to my computer and looked at sites relating to the 1968 Democratic National Convention in Chicago. After an hour of hopscotching from site to site, I found what I was looking for in an archive about the antiwar movement.

It was titled "The Leader Who Wasn't There."

> *One small group of demonstrators was driven into a near frenzy of antiwar rage after they listened to a fiery speech by a young graduate student. Duncan Delgado, 20, of San Francisco, exhorted the crowd to storm the police barricades around the hotels housing many of the delegates.*
>
> *"Death to all pig cops and the corrupt politicians who back them. Death to an administration in Washington that sends its soldier goons to kill innocents in Vietnam. Death to all Caucasian mercenaries with Asian blood dripping off their bayonets—may they be castrated and their balls hung out to dry on the iron gates of respectable world opinion."*
>
> *At that, the crowd of twenty-five or so high school and college-age students began to chant, "Hey, hey, LBJ. How many kids did you kill today?"*

Then, each picked up a candle being handed out by people on the edge of the park and lighted it before forming a single line, ready to walk down the street.

At a signal from their organizers, the ragtag group began slowly to advance on the first barricade, two blocks away. As they moved out, others along the way joined them, forming into two more lines. This reporter looked for Delgado, the man who had started it all, to be leading the march. I ran along the sidelines to a point where I was ahead of the first rank of marchers.

But Delgado was nowhere to be seen. Instead, their leader seemed to be a beautiful young woman dressed in an Army field jacket and combat boots and carrying an expensive-looking camera.

— By Ezra Beekman

The next morning, I decided to drive to the Oregon coast where I own a small house north of Newport near the Yaquina Head Lighthouse. I have been going there for twenty years, since I joined the faculty at Oregon University.

If I am well-known on campus because of the long years I've worked there, I am equally well-known on the central coast for other, less highfalutin' reasons. Because of my penchant for nosing into things that don't really concern me—an old reporter's curse—I have been involved in the solution of more than one murder. One, at the Yaquina Head Lighthouse, involved the death of a friend. The other included international politics, the killing of whales, and the carcass of a Gray whale that washed ashore right behind my house.

Although my policewoman friend Angela Pride kids me about my "cases," I'd rather think of them as incidents, where I was just trying to help as any public-spirited citizen would do.

I can just hear Angela's retort to that line of reasoning. "Yeah. Right. Try telling that to Art Cutler!"

The county sheriff does seem to dislike me intensely. I guess it might be because I once caused him to lose his job. But I was only trying to help a friend clear her name. Ever since that incident—involving the blowing up of a whale carcass—Kutler had gone out of his way to implicate me in all unsolved crimes in the area.

I pulled into the driveway of my house just after noon. I dropped my bag and briefcase just inside the door and headed straight for the beach. By walking north, it was possible to descend the steep incline to the sand below. This particular stretch of beach led to the lighthouse itself, about a mile away.

I slipped off my shoes and socks and rolled up my jeans so I wouldn't have to worry about getting them wet. There was nothing like the feel of the ocean hitting your legs and the sand between your toes. All my life, the ocean had relaxed me. All stress seemed to drain from my body as soon as I got near it. Today, the sun was so warm I started sweating. Before long, I took off my sweatshirt and tied it around my waist, just like in junior high.

Ahead of me, the tall column of the lighthouse loomed, its white walls shimmering in the bright sunlight. Every once in a while, the light from on top would skitter by. That light had been burning continuously since 1872. For me the structure represented stability and durability in a world too prone to the transitory and the temporary.

Far down the beach, someone was walking toward me. This was unusual. Because of the difficulty of getting here from above, few people come down here. That was why I liked it so much.

I bent down to pick up some broken pieces of shell. I discarded most of them and then spied a rock in the shape of a whale. I collected these tiny, natural good-luck pieces. Was it the sea giving me a gift by battering and polishing this flotsam of the land? I placed two such objects in the pocket of my jeans.

When the figure was within sight, I couldn't believe my eyes.

"Maxine March? I can't believe it!"

She batted her beautiful eyes a few times, but seemed to be faking her surprise. "What are you doing here?"

"Well, I'm not stalking you. I live here." I turned and pointed back the other way. "My weekend house is on that bluff."

"Wow. Looks like a great place. Want to sit down?"

I nodded, and we both walked up a slight incline to the large boulders resting against the cliffside. I brushed hers off before she sat down.

"Thanks. That's thoughtful of you. No one has so much as pulled out a chair . . ."

". . . or dusted off a rock."

We both laughed.

"Yeah, in many, many years."

We talked for a long time about a lot of things—our pasts, the present, our likes and dislikes in everything from food to movies to music.

I felt a chill in the air as the sun began sinking behind Yaquina Head. I handed my sweatshirt to her, and she pulled it over her head and tugged it into place.

"You got plans for tonight?" she asked. "I'm sorry. I want you to know that I don't make a habit of hitting on my professors."

We both got to our feet and stood facing one another.

"Come on," she said. "Show me your house."

Then she took hold of my pants and, tugging on them in front, led me toward my house.

*   *   *

"Nice place. You owned it long?"

We had barely stepped inside the door of my house, a modest two-bedroom cottage that was long on view, but short on square footage.

"About ten years or so. I rented it at first, then got a chance to buy it from another faculty member at the university. I decided I'd rather have a house here than in Corvallis. I own a small condo there."

"Mr. Money Bags," she said over her shoulder.

Maxine was walking around the house quickly, glancing at pictures, picking up books. She hadn't seemed so hyper when I met her on campus the day before.

"Want something to drink?" I asked, hoping she would settle down.

"Any kind of soft drink will do. Right out of the can is okay."

I got two Pepsis out of the refrigerator and popped open the tabs on top.

"Let's sit in here." I motioned toward the living room.

She followed me and sat down in a chair.

"Thanks. Sorry. I guess I'm being obnoxious. I get agitated now and again. The doctor calls it an anxiety attack. I've had them for years. Comes from being married to a man like Duncan. He'd drive anybody totally nuts. Just thinking about him makes my skin crawl. He is one screwed-up guy, believe me. If I told the university hierarchy what I know, he'd be finished."

I enjoy gossip as much as the next guy, but this was making me uneasy. Even though I had invited her here, Maxine was making me nervous. Technically, she was not my student. She had only come to my office to ask for advice. But here she was, stomping around my house after showing up unexpectedly. While I was no psychologist, she seemed pretty agitated to me. And rather unpredictable.

"You know, Maxine, I hate to be rude, but I've got to drive into Newport to run some errands. It's gotten later than I thought." I made a big thing about looking at my watch.

"Oh, I thought we could talk for a while. I'd really like to get to know you better."

"I'd like that too, but I've got things to do. I'm sorry." Not that I didn't want to know more of her, in the biblical sense. She had a figure most women her age would die for—or, at least, starve for.

I got up, but she didn't budge from the chair. She slipped off my sweatshirt, leaving only a tight T-shirt to cover her great body.

"Seem hot and stuffy in here, Tom?"

I was getting hot too, but not from any stuffiness in the room. She pressed the can to her forehead.

"Whew. That's better. I don't suppose you'd want to cool off with me—like, back there?"

She pointed toward the hall that led to my bedroom.

"No, I don't suppose I would. Look, Maxine. I feel awkward about where you think this is going. I'm a faculty member of a university you might attend. You might take a course from me. It's just not a good idea to get involved in any way but professionally. We barely know one another. How do you know I wouldn't treat you like Duncan did?" I was really reaching here to come up with an excuse she wouldn't take offense at.

"You're too nice a guy for that. You'd be kind and gentle with me, I know you would." Then she started to cry.

I handed her a box of tissue, then retreated to where I had been standing across the room. She blew her nose loudly.

"Why don't you like me?"

"I do like you, but I can't help you with the kind of problems you apparently have. I'm not a psychologist."

"You think I'm nuts?" The tears stopped and her eyes hardened.

"No, not at all. You're just upset." How was I going to get rid of her?

She stood and walked over to me. "You are such a sexy guy. And a nice guy." She put her arms around my neck and hugged me tightly. I kept my hands at my sides. Then she took my head in her hands and pushed me back gently.

"You are just the kind of guy a girl dreams about. The kind of guy to take home to mother."

"Your mother lives around here—Portland, Corvallis?" I was stalling for time.

"My mother is dead! I was only using a figure of speech. My mother got cancer and died when I was fifteen. My dad remarried in less than a year. My stepmother didn't like me, and I didn't like her. I left as soon as I was eighteen. We lost touch, but when he died last year, that bitch had the nerve to call and ask me to pay for the funeral." She shook her head in disbelief.

"And did you?"

"Yeah. I asked Duncan for the money, and he gave it to me. He has that old-world thing about honoring your family. But I didn't go to the funeral."

She dropped her arms, walked over to the breakfast bar, and sat on a stool.

"So, why don't I wait here for you and then scramble us some eggs. I make good eggs with cheese and salsa. Got any salsa?"

"I can't do it. I've got other plans."

Her face clouded over, and she started to cry again, this time without the heavy sobs.

"Don't you find me attractive? I'm really attractive when I slip into something more comfortable. You got a big, snuggly robe?"

I ignored the question and reached for my sweatshirt.

"You might want to put this back on. It gets chilly by late afternoon. You can keep it."

A knock at the door interrupted our verbal sparring.

As I walked to the door, she made a sudden movement. Already turning the knob, I did not see in time that she had pulled off her T-shirt.

"Angela."

I glanced behind to see Maxine in all her bare-breasted glory.

"Er . . . a . . . er. . . . Come in."

ngela's smile at finding me home quickly faded when she stepped into the room and saw the topless Maxine March standing behind me. Even though we were no longer a "couple," it probably upset her to think that someone else had taken her place. Except that no one else had taken her place. It just looked that way. What she was seeing was so far from the truth that I wasn't even embarrassed—except for Maxine.

"Angela. Great to see you. Come in."

I kissed her on the mouth and extended my hug to more than the usual perfunctory brevity. I wanted to make a point with Maxine. Angela seemed surprised at my passion, but went along with it.

"I'm obviously interrupting something here, Tom. I drove over for the day and decided to see if you could give a girl a cup of coffee."

"You bet I can. Sit down."

I glanced at Maxine, who had pulled on her T-shirt and my sweatshirt. Then I did something I almost never do. I was rude.

"Ms. March was just leaving."

Maxine looked sheepish, as she walked toward the door.

"Thanks for your time, Professor Martindale. I'll let you know if I decide to take your class." Her statement was so counter to what had just been happening it was ludicrous. But I didn't laugh.

"Okay, Ms. March. That will be fine. Maybe I will see you around the department."

She turned and walked out the door. I hadn't seen her car so wasn't sure how she got here or could get away. But I didn't care. I went into the kitchen to make the coffee.

"So, Tom. Do you audition all your students this way—I mean the female ones?" Angela was smiling through her sarcasm.

"It isn't how it looked," I said, as I placed the cups on the table between our chairs. "It's a somewhat long story, but . . ."

"I'm not on duty, and I've got all evening. I'm all ears, as they say."

"I hadn't met her until she came to my office yesterday to ask about one of my classes. Then, she showed up here on the beach this afternoon while I was walking and insisted we come to my house, and you know the rest."

"You skipped the part about her slipping into something more comfortable. Was she demonstrating some new writing technique?"

Angela was sounding jealous. Given our past history together, I wasn't sure if I liked that or not, but our discussion was interrupted by a knock on the door. I opened it to find Maxine. She rushed into the room looking worried.

"I left something here."

Another sweatshirt? A bra?

"My camera. I had it with me when I came in."

"Is this it?" said Angela, as she held up the camera. "It was in the cushion of this chair."

"Thanks. God, I was afraid I'd lost that, too. It means a lot to me."

She took the camera from Angela's outstretched hand and clutched it to her chest.

"Glad you found it," I said, gently pushing Maxine toward the still-open door. I closed it behind her and then turned the deadbolt.

"That was pretty rude, Tom."

"That woman is strange. You know I'm usually a polite guy, but something about her scares me. Did you see that look on her face? She is spacey. I do *not* need someone like that in my life!"

"She is quite a looker, Tom. All that beauty could make a man overlook other shortcomings." Angela was mocking me, but I didn't care. Her tone lightened my mood considerably.

"Better spacey than uptight and overly pressed," I replied with a straight face. We always joked about how organized and neat she was—or at least, I did. She was a bit sensitive about the subject, and it might have had something to do with our breakup.

"Okay. A truce." She held up both hands. "Go on with your story."

"There's not much else to tell. We were just talking here when we got to the house and she proceeded to pull off her clothes at the same time you knocked on the door."

"More than a little odd. What do you know about her?"

"She's divorced from a faculty member at the university. Duncan Delgado in biology."

"The name is familiar."

"They met in Chicago in the sixties. He was a radical, and she was a radical groupie, I gather."

"How'd you find out all of that?"

"She told me."

"On your first meeting, she spilled her proverbial guts to you?" Angela was shaking her head.

"You know, Angela—my honest face and all." I framed my face in my hands and moved my head from side to side.

"I remember Delgado now. We had a complaint against him from a female student. For sexual harassment, as I recall. About a year ago." She thought for a minute. "Said he pinned her to the wall in a lab one night."

"That doesn't sound like sexual harassment. It sounds like assault. Did you talk to him?"

"We tried, but he was out of the country attending a conference when we stopped by his office for a chat. By the time he returned, the woman had dropped the charges."

"What was her name?"

"Why do you want to know that?"

"Er . . . a . . . thought I might have had her in class, that's all."

"Melanie Santiago, I think it was."

"Doesn't ring a bell." I made a mental note of it all the same.

"I really hate that kind of thing. I think it's a total betrayal of the trust most students have for us as their professors. I assume there was an age difference?"

"Yeah, a big one. Maybe she couldn't resist him, Latin to Latin," she said.

"He is nice-looking," I said.

"You know him?"

"We met quite by accident a couple of weeks ago. We had jury duty together. He made the final cut; I did not. We talked a bit while we were waiting to be called."

"Which case?"

"Let's see. Some Hispanic guy. Hector Morales, I think his name was. Killed a jewelry store owner in an attempted robbery."

"Oh, yeah. The trial was over before it began."
"Why was that?"
"He escaped from jail."

I didn't think much more about Duncan Delgado, Maxine March, or Hector Morales all summer. I had to concentrate on organizing the presidential search process.

Once money had been transferred into the special presidential search account, I started to spend it. For me, the first step was to work out a position description that could be presented to the search committee at its first meeting. I thought it better to give them something to hack away at than waiting for members to develop one from scratch.

It took the most of one day to develop an ad, which I planned to run in *The New York Times*, the *Wall Street Journal*, *The Oregonian*, and *The Chronicle of Higher Education*.

President
Oregon University
A public research university and member of a seven-campus system of higher education, Oregon University is a land grant, sea grant, and space grant institution. Founded in

1868, Oregon University aims to achieve openness, social responsibility, and inquiry, as well as excellent academic programs and superior educational experiences for its undergraduate and graduate students. For its faculty, it aims for an atmosphere of creative scholarship.

The State Board of Higher Education invites applications and nominations for the position of president. The president is the chief executive officer of the university and reports to the board.

The president must be an experienced and successful leader and good communicator, a person who has a record of visionary and dynamic leadership. Specifically the candidate for the position is expected to bring the following:

- A knowledge of global, national, and regional trends in higher education and state economic development
- The administrative and managerial experience and skills necessary to lead a complex organization
- Interpersonal skills that will foster a sense of community and common purpose with all university constituencies
- A record of success in strategic planning, leadership, budget preparation, and fiscal management
- Political skills in dealing with the executive and legislative leaders of a state or city
- An understanding of the role of new technology in education
- Understanding of campus culture, including faculty governance and faculty/student interaction
- Experience in, and a commitment to, promoting diversity
- A successful record of working with business and federal and state agencies to obtain research support and funding for capital projects

The minimum qualifications are an earned doctorate and experience appropriate for the institution. Interested individuals should send a letter of interest, curriculum vitae, and contact information for five references.

What a bunch of academic gobbledygook! I knew I needed to throw in words like "diversity" and "openness." I also wanted to put in boilerplate stuff about the university, along with minimum requirements for the job. But this ad seemed way too long. It was hard to come up with the catchy phrase all mainstream ads aim for. The information was the message, and people had to know what we wanted. I knew, by experience, though, that unqualified people would still apply, attempting to stretch their backgrounds and credentials to fit.

I decided the best thing to do was to give the ad to the committee before our first meeting and let them start revising it. Although it was their role to do so, I dreaded the time it would take.

* * *

"I am pleased to call to order the first meeting of the presidential search committee." Dimitri Chekhov started the meeting on time at 10 A.M. "I am honored to have been chosen to chair, and I will attempt to create an atmosphere of openness and honesty in our deliberations. I am available to you all at any time. My office and home numbers are in your binders. We are pleased to have as vice-chair Hadley Collins, vice president for public affairs."

Hadley raised her hand.

"As board secretary and chief administrative officer, we are happy to have Tom Martindale, professor of journalism."

I also waved, but did not get up from my chair.

"You may know of Tom's various exploits as an amateur detective."

There was a smattering of giggles and nodding of heads. My face got hot. Why had all of these past incidents been so public? I really hate it all the publicity. It did nothing to help my academic career.

"I would like each of you to introduce yourselves as we go around the table. And, I almost forgot. Thank you so much for serving on this important committee. We all get committee assignments, some good, some bad, some meaningful, some superfluous. This, ladies and gentlemen, is a big one. We will help determine the course of this university over the next few years."

He nodded at the man to his right, a youthful-looking guy with long hair fashioned into a ponytail.

"Hello. I'm Chad Nunn, a professor of oceanography."

I detected an Australian accent. Oceanography seemed to attract a lot of people from that country.

"I'll do my best to uphold the dignity of the British Empire."

Loud laughs rang out as he sat down.

"I'm Liz Stein, associate professor of political science."

Liz and I had been on another committee a few years before. I was glad to see that she had toned down her revolutionary look of blue work shirt, jeans, sandals, and a bandanna on her head. Instead, she had on slacks and a tasteful sweater.

"I want to look out for people of color here. I mean, both in the candidates and what the candidates think. We need a president with a feminist agenda. In fact, we need a woman president!"

Dead silence greeted her little outburst. Her passion, though undoubtedly heartfelt, was misplaced at this point in the scheme of things.

"My goodness. I'm not sure what kind of agenda that is, dear."

Liz glared at the speaker.

"I'm Gloria Gordon. I used to be president of the University Alumni Association. I must say I don't feel downtrodden or repressed at all, dear."

"Don't call me dear," muttered Liz under her breath.

Ms. Gordon did not seem to hear Liz, as she fingered her gold necklace. She was wearing one of those knubby suits that are made by Chanel or Versace or some foreign designer. Every strand of her blonde hair was in place, and she was wearing very large glasses.

"I hope we can hire someone to make us proud to be a part of this wonderful university. I met my husband here. He was a Delt, and I was an Alpha Phi. What magic days we had—and we didn't need the Trysting Tree to fall in love."

"Oh, please," muttered Liz, at Ms. Gordon's mention of a tree on lower campus—long since felled by lightning—where the guys and gals of old used to go, in the vernacular of the time, to "spoon."

Gloria Gordon kept smiling and acted as if she hadn't heard Liz Stein.

Chekhov rescued things by moving on. "Thanks, Gloria, for your wise words. Good for all of us to remember why we're here."

Liz was pouting by this time, but said nothing. It was one thing to mouth off to an outsider, but quite another to defy a senior professor, even one from a department not her own. She would be up for promotion to full professor someday, and one never knew who might be on one's committee down the road.

"Professor Gomez."

"Buenos días, amigos," said Miguel Gomez of Hispanic Studies. He was tall and thin and good-looking. I was sure the girls in his classes swooned over his sad brown eyes and care-

fully trimmed mustache and goatee. I had heard he was happily married and had four children.

"I, too, am pleased to be a part of this important undertaking. I only hope we will consider any people of color who might apply."

"You got that right, man." Ricky Lee Washington was sitting across from Gomez in the middle of the table, so everyone heard what he said. He was a short, good-looking black man with his hair worn in tight cornrows. He had a blue stud in the lobe of his right ear.

"Mr. Washington," said Chekhov. "I would ask you to wait your turn to speak."

"Sorry, man. I got carried away in the moment."

"Anything else, Professor Gomez?"

"No, sir, that's all I wanted to say."

"Very well. We will go to Alex Crandell next."

"What about me?" said Washington in a louder than necessary voice. "Am I sliced bread or what?"

"You will wait your turn, young man. I am in charge of this meeting!"

"So that's the way this group's gonna play out, eh pops? All the whites get to speak, then the rest of us throw in a few yes'ems and no'ems!"

Both Washington and Chekhov were angry by this time. Things were not getting off to a very harmonious start. Hadley and I exchanged glances and then she spoke.

"Maybe this is a good time for a break."

She got up before Chekhov could say anything and walked to a rear door of the conference room. She opened it and a waiter pushed in a cart containing coffee, tea, soft drinks, and a tray of cookies. Members got up and were soon clustered around the cart making their drink and cookie selections.

"Nice save," I muttered to Hadley when I passed her. She kept going to Washington's side and motioned for him to join her at the far end of the room. Dimitri Chekhov headed for me.

"Impudent young man," he whispered.

"I think students feel outnumbered and overwhelmed by the rest of us. It would be fairly daunting, don't you think, Dimitri?"

"That is all well and good, Thomas, but I will not allow discourtesy. Young people have to respect their elders!"

"I agree," I said, although I really didn't. "But we've got to make them a part of the process. They do represent a large constituency of the university. I mean, nearly twenty thousand students have to count for something. I think Mr. Washington compensates for his minority status—both as a student in a committee full of faculty and as a Black student who is outnumbered—by being quick to speak and quick to anger. I'm no psychologist, but I think it's a defense mechanism on his part. What do you think, Dimitri?"

"Well, Thomas. I guess you may have a point. But it will erode my authority if I allow myself to be bullied by someone less than half my age. I cannot abide discourtesy!"

"Just give him a little leeway, Dimitri. That's all I ask. Try killing him with kindness. If you bend over backwards being fair and he still defies you, the rest of us will be on your side and ostracize him for you."

"I take your point. Very well. I will try it your way, Thomas. At least for a while."

Because of the time I spent talking to Dimitri, I had only a few minutes to grab a soft drink and an oatmeal cookie before returning to my seat. Hadley and I nodded to one another slightly across the table. We would soon see if our efforts had paid off.

"Mr. Washington, I think I would like to hear from you next, if you don't mind," purred Chekhov with a thin smile.

Washington finished downing a cookie and took a gulp of coffee before speaking.

"Thank you, sir. I appreciate it. I appreciate your kind courtesy. Victoria Chen and me, we represent thousands of students. We take that role seriously, very seriously. The fact should not be lost on any of you that we are from two important minorities here on campus. I take that role seriously, too—and so does Vicki." He looked toward the diminutive young lady sitting at the end of the table, and she nodded her head in agreement. "Students are important to this university. In many ways, we are the university. What it all boils down to is pretty simple: what we become reflects credit on this place. If you all prepare us for the world, we will make you proud. That's all we want—to make all of you, and our mommas and papas, proud."

"Well put, Ricky," said Hadley. Everyone else nodded in agreement, even Chekhov.

"I can second what Mr. Washington said emphatically. I'm Alex Crandell, a 1975 graduate in political science. I'm an attorney in Portland, and I represent the State Board of Education. Any success I have had in my career comes from my parents and this university. I enter this important committee assignment with that thought foremost in my mind. That's all I have to say."

"Miss Chen?"

"Thank you, Professor Chekhov. One of the best things about speaking last is that you don't have to say too much because all the good stuff has been said already. I'm in that position now. Let me just second the words that Ricky uttered, and add that I take my role as a woman here seriously."

"Amen to that," said Liz Stein loudly.

"Well, that's great," said Chekhov. "I think we're going to have a fine time here, along with our very serious assignment. You've got your board packets with our schedule. We'll be leaving the heavy lifting to Tom Martindale to bring us some people to consider and to keep us on schedule. At that, we stand adjourned."

ix weeks later, we were in the doldrums of summer, a rather hot summer. As happened every year, the campus and the town seemed pretty empty. Because many students earn the money to pay their tuition during that period, three-fourths of the students leave. Although I missed the excitement and bustle these young people brought to everything they did, it was nice to have a break from all of that. And I wasn't teaching, either.

My newfound freedom gave me plenty of time to work on search committee business. First, I set up our committee members in groups as follows: Dimitri in charge of Liz Stein, Victoria Chen, and Miguel Gomez; Hadley with Ricky Washington and Gloria Gordon; and I would be overseeing Alex Crandell and Chad Nunn.

The advertisements and individual nominations had brought in a deluge of candidates—over two hundred. I broke the stack into three groups, and I asked the committee

to read the files and cull people who were obviously unqualified. Then, I asked them to rank numerically the remaining
people by three main criteria: experience, leadership, vision.
The process went so well that we had reduced the group to
seventy-five candidates in a week, then twenty-five in another
ten days.

In any wide-ranging search for people to fill a job opening
at almost any level, you always wind up with people who try to
tailor their experience to fit the position. Sometimes the stretch
is obvious, as when people who have spent their entire professional lives doing one thing suddenly apply to do something
they obviously have no ability to do.

Many of the dossiers we got were from people with little or
no experience at running any large company or organization,
let alone a complex institution like a university. Just having a
Ph.D. and a desire to advance into the higher realms of academic administration was not enough; people had to have
been chairs of departments and/or deans of colleges, or have
held the job of provost.

The exception to this rule was anyone who had made it in
politics, the military, or maybe big business. If such a person
was well-known, the cachet of notoriety might outweigh a lack
of experience; being in the news for years because of this other
work—say a senate seat or a cabinet position or even a military
command—might just be enough. The media at the university's various publics might respond so well that having the
specific experience of running a university might not matter—
their fame could help them raise money, while someone else
ran the university day to day.

*   *   *

While the subcommittees were narrowing down their final-ist lists, I made another trip to the courthouse. After calling ahead for an appointment, I once again climbed the stairs to Judge Andrews's court room. As she had predicted, the cere-mony for granting adoptions to several happy couples was just ending. The room that was so often filled with sadness, anxi-ety, and menace was now warmed by beaming adults and beautiful babies. Just as I walked in the door, she finished this process, and the fifty or so parents, grandparents, and other family members and friends began applauding the smiling judge. She thanked them and wished them good luck in their new lives together.

Then, as the laughing and chatting throng moved out the door, she motioned for me to come forward. Going against the flow, I walked into the milling crowd and through the swing-ing gate.

"Mr. Martindale. I recognized you from your time on the jury," she said, as she stepped down from the bench.

"It must be a nice break for you, I mean making all these people so happy."

"It really is. I usually see people at their worst. Come on back."

I followed her through a door she opened by inserting a card in a slot, just like the system used by hotels. Behind the scenes, the courthouse was as neat and orderly as in the courtroom itself. To the left, a counter separated three clerks who were sit-ting at desks and staring at computer screens.

The judge stopped to consult with her clerk about the after-noon's docket, then motioned for me to follow her up the car-peted stairs to her chambers. The restoration of the building had extended behind the scenes: the wood paneling went part-way up the walls, and the carpeting seemed vintage to me.

The third floor housed only the judges' offices. Judge Andrews's chamber was a large square room in the left corner overlooking the jail. The desk, conference table, chairs, and old-fashioned stacker bookshelves were all oak, befitting the late nineteenth-century look of the entire building.

"Sit down," she said, as she took off her black robe, and hung it on a freestanding rack near her desk. "Whew! What a morning!" she said, finally sitting down. "So what can I do for you?"

I had come for two reasons—one honest, the other a bit dishonest. The former was really a subterfuge for the latter, as I did the easy part first.

"Judge Andrews, I teach a course in public affairs reporting each winter term, and I wondered if I could bring my students in to observe your courtroom and then have you brief them on what you do. Later some of them might follow up by interviewing you to gather material for a profile."

"I'd be delighted to have them. I consider it part of my duties as a judge to explain the operation of the court system to the public. What better way than through a group of eager young journalists-to-be!"

"Thank you. I'd hoped you'd be willing to let us in. Maybe we can talk at the start of the term next January to see what cases you've got coming up that might be interesting."

"Sure. That would work for me."

"I should mention that all of the students won't be doing a profile of you. I won't subject you to that! Public affairs also covers business and science and other branches of government, plus the police. The kids will be covering them like a beat. Are you familiar with the old beat system a lot of newspapers use?"

"Yes, I am. I took a couple of journalism courses in college. I know exactly what you're talking about."

"Great. Do you get many reporters in your courtroom?" I was stalling as a way of putting off my main reason for asking to see the judge. I did want her to host my class, but I could have set that up over the telephone.

"Maybe every month or so. It depends on the sensational nature of the case. It usually takes a murder trial to bring the TV crews down from Portland or up from Eugene. I don't mind as long as they abide by the rules and don't disrupt the proceedings."

"Does it change the atmosphere at all?"

Sometimes it does, yes. I find myself wondering how I look on film—too thin or too fat or if my hair is combed." She smiled. "And some of the attorneys tend to preen a bit more than normal. It's never as bad as on big cases, like those involving celebrities in California. Attorneys on both sides tend to get out of control down there."

"Yeah, so do judges."

"No comment on that," she laughed. "I'd better take the Fifth Amendment."

"Judge Andrews, I wanted to ask you about something else."

"Sure. What is that?" She pulled off her glasses and smiled.

"The defendant in that trial you conducted a month or so ago, where I was in the jury pool, but not selected . . ."

"Hector Morales."

"Yes, that's the name."

"What about it?"

"I heard that he escaped from custody. Is that true?"

"Yes, I'm afraid he did. It was very embarrassing for the Sheriff's Department. The state police are still investigating, but it looks like someone helped him, someone from the outside."

"That must be a rare thing. I mean, it's like something in a movie."

"Yeah, a movie with a bad ending—at least for the sheriff. A deputy got fired, and we're tightening procedures."

"So Morales is still at large?"

"As far as I know. He probably went back to Mexico. The border is so porous, people go back and forth all the time, despite all the money that's spent on the border patrol and fences."

I hesitated a moment, then said, "I'll admit I had another reason for asking. In the past few months, I've come to know someone else who was on that jury panel. But he got picked."

She looked at me expectantly. "And that would be?"

"Sorry for the dramatic pauses. I'm hesitating because I don't want to stir something up that might mean nothing."

"Look, Mr. Martindale . . ."

"Tom, Your Honor."

"Okay, Tom. And I can be Betty when we're out of the courtroom."

"Deal."

"If you know something that bears on the Morales escape, you are obligated by law to tell me. I took an oath to abide by the laws of this state." She motioned toward the flag of Oregon resting in a floor pedestal across the room. "You are a citizen of the state, and there are laws about reporting crimes to the proper authorities. I am a member of the latter category."

Her smile had faded by this time, and she sat there staring at me.

"No, I don't know anything about the escape. It's about the juror, Duncan Delgado. He's a big-time scientist on campus. At one point in the jury selection process, when Morales was being led in, I saw him exchange glances with Delgado and Delgado looked kind of scared."

She shook her head. "Pardon me for doubting you, Tom, but it is a bit of a stretch to think that a long-time gangbanger

would know a college professor, let alone be afraid of him."
She smiled at the ridiculousness of the thought.

"I saw what I saw."

"And I think you've been reading too many legal thrillers."

"There's something else, Judge. Delgado's former wife is taking a class from me—or planning to. She's told me some pretty kinky things about him. He was an antiwar activist in the 1960s."

"So was I," said the judge. "Since when is that a crime, except to the Right Wing? I'm just not sure what you're saying, Tom."

"I guess I'm not either. I just got a sense that Morales and Delgado knew one another."

"Guilt by Hispanic association?" she laughed.

She was right to be skeptical, but I was getting a bit miffed at her mocking tone. I decided not to pursue it then nor say anything more about Maxine March.

"Look, I've taken enough of your time. I just thought I'd mention it. It is pretty harebrained, I'll admit." I got up to leave.

"Look, Tom. I didn't mean to seem to be making fun of you. I'll make some inquiries. This investigation is ongoing. We need to look at everything and everybody."

I moved toward the door. "I was just curious. You said Hector Morales was a gangbanger?"

"Yeah, since he was a kid. Born in Mexico and, let's see, I have the case file right here since the investigation is under way." She opened a thick file and began to turn the pages inside. I sat down again in a chair opposite her. "Here it is. His family migrated to Chicago when he was a baby. He grew up there in the projects, then his father was killed in some kind of gunfight around the time of the Democratic Convention in 1968. No details of that in here. Then his mother was deported with her four children, including Hector. Back in Mexico, he never went to school, but was considered very smart. Set up a street gang in Tijuana that specialized in robbing jewelry stores. That's what he was trying to do here, before he allegedly shot the owner."

"But how'd he get from way down there to way up here?"

"That's the mystery. These guys usually come to a place where others have gone before—a relative, a friend, someone who has a job or a place to stay. Then they branch out from there. Morales did this crime alone." She kept turning pages in the file. "Yes. No one else involved. And no one came forward to support him. That's unusual. In my experience, when a Mexican national goes on trial, one or two family members come in or hire an attorney to represent the defendant. It didn't happen here."

"Who represented him? That guy that threw me off the jury?"

"He's a very good attorney from Salem—Lorenzo Madrid. Like the city in Spain."

"How could Morales afford to hire him?"

"Pro bono. Madrid did it for free. He does that all the time. Oregon gets a huge number of illegal migrants passing through each year, following the crops. You ever drive up Highway 99W on the way to Aurora? There are lots of farms where they work. Inevitably, some of these people get into trouble with the law. Madrid reads the papers and often steps into these cases. I suppose he read about Hector Morales and stepped forward. The rest of the time he does a lot of corporate work. He's a very good attorney."

I stood up again. "Thanks for your time, Judge Andrews. I'll be in touch about the class."

I waited until I was back on the street before I jotted down Lorenzo Madrid's name in a small notebook I carry around for such purposes.

The next day, I called a meeting of the subcommittee I had placed myself in charge of, deferring to them on time and place. After a series of at least twenty phone calls, voice mail messages, and e-mails, we agreed to meet in Crandell's law offices in Portland on a day when Nunn would be passing through town on the way to an oceanography conference in France.

On the day of the meeting, Chad Nunn was already in the elegant waiting room when I stepped off the elevator.

"His secretary tells me he's on his way out," smiled Nunn.

As a partner in one of Portland's most prestigious law firms, Crandell probably made more money than Nunn's and my salary combined. But he didn't let that show as he walked briskly over to the two of us and shook hands.

"Chad. Tom. Come on back."

We followed him into a maze of cubicles and workstations, passing large offices with expensive-looking furniture and

floor-to-ceiling windows with great views of the Portland skyline, the Willamette River, and Mount Hood. He stopped at an
open door and motioned us to go in before him.

"Coffee?"

We both nodded. He stepped to a phone.

"Clare, some coffee, please."

Although he had his coat off, Crandell was dressed in an elegant gray pinstripe suit. His pale yellow shirt was set off by a
silk tie, also yellow with red scales of justice as a design. He
looked to be in his early fifties.

I had worn a coat and tie, but Nunn had on chinos, a polo
shirt, and a blue windbreaker with some kind of oceanic-look-
ing emblem on the front. He seemed to be the kind of guy who
didn't let anyone intimidate him, no matter how well-dressed
or imposing.

Before long, a beautiful woman walked in the door carrying
a tray bearing a large coffee pot, cups and plates, and a plate
piled high with croissants.

"Clare. This is Professor Nunn and Professor Martindale. My
colleagues in this search committee business."

We both got to our feet to shake her hand.

"Clare Norman is my assistant. I wouldn't know the time of
day if it weren't for Clare." He gave her arm a squeeze as he got
up to pass the pastries around.

"Great to meet you. Is there anything else, Mr. Crandell?"

"No, I think not. Hold everybody at bay for a few hours.
Okay, my dear?"

She smiled and nodded and closed the door on her way out.

"Wonderfully talented girl. She came here wanting to be a
paralegal, but I've got bigger plans for her than that! So, what
have you got for us, Tom?"

I opened my briefcase and pulled out ten dossiers I had assembled with the help of Hadley's secretary and the search firm we had hired to screen the applicants.

"You know you always get some ringers when you advertise nationally like we did."

I handed duplicate files on six people to the two of them, plus a list of the names of the ten we had rejected outright. I reread the material, and they looked it over for the first time. The room was completely silent for ten minutes, the only sound coming from the ticking of a large grandfather clock at the head of a long conference table. Even though its age and stately appearance was in sharp contrast to the clear glass table and black leather chairs, it looked as though it belonged.

"My grandfather's clock," said Crandell, when he saw me looking at it. "He founded this firm, and I keep it to remind me of where I came from. It keeps me grounded and linked to a family past I am very proud of. Plus, it keeps perfect time."

"It's really beautiful," I said.

"Makes you long for the days when not every timepiece was digital with a chip up its ass to keep it running," said Nunn, shaking his head at the thought.

"I should think you'd have all kinds of ways to tell time at sea, Dr. Nunn."

"Nothing beats a watch," he answered, pointing to his left wrist.

"Well, then, I guess we need to get to it. More coffee, gentlemen?"

We both nodded, and he filled our cups. I took the lull in conversation as time to help myself to another croissant.

"First of all, do either of you see a name you recognize on the list of people we will not consider? Or a job title or background that seems like a fit?"

"Seems like people who are just too far away from what we want," said Nunn. "A former concert pianist who teaches music at a college, an army colonel now in private industry, the owner of a minor-league baseball team, an actress who now heads an arts lobbying group. I can't see any of them filling the bill for us."

"The actress might have possibilities," said Crandell. "I mean, we've got to strengthen the liberal arts at OU. I speak from experience. I was a poli-sci/pre-law major."

"I agree with you on that, Mr. Crandell," I said. "I think she got bounced from the skills matrix because she lacked any administrative experience. She's never managed anyone else. I think an executive director runs the lobbying group. She's the spokesperson who has the name to get them in the door."

"Yeah, I see that," said Crandell. "Probably best not to pursue her. I guess I'd seen some of her films. That interested me. I wanted the chance to talk to her in person and ask if it was true that she once slept with Robert Redford." Crandell laughed loudly, and so did Nunn and I.

"So we can move on to those we might consider?"

Crandell and Nunn nodded.

"In alphabetical order: Margo Baines, Harrison Andrews Johnson, Joseph Henry Niles, Alexander Shay, Joseph Svoboda, and Lillian White.

"Why do you academics always need three names?" laughed Crandell, shaking his head ruefully. "In my line of work, only people arrested for committing a crime rate three names—right from their rap sheet."

"They think it sounds more important," said Nunn. "It's all a bunch of academic bullshit."

"Maybe they think it looks better on their books and articles," I added.

"Whatever," said Crandell, somewhat dismissively. "It just seems odd. It just seems odd."

"That it does," I said. "That it does."

I picked up the top file on the stack and opened it. "Margo Baines, vice provost for academic affairs at the University of Delaware."

They opened their identical folders.

"In that job for three years. Department chair for six years before that. Taught in a number of schools around the country for ten years."

"Is that normal?" asked Crandell, "I mean, to stay in jobs for such a short time? Such a short time?"

"Yes, it is," I said. "You probably want people who will stay here for the rest of their working lives. In the academic world, the jobs you hold and where you hold them is deemed more important than how long you work wherever you work."

"Yeah. That's right," added Nunn. "That's just one of the many anomalies in academe."

"So, what do we think of Ms. Baines?"

"Very impressive, very impressive," said Crandell.

Was I being unfair or did the distinguished attorney have an anomaly of his own? He repeated things he had just said. I suppose he did this for emphasis, like he was talking to a jury.

"She's got some overseas posts that I wonder about," said Nunn. "It's harder to check them out because of the distance and language problems, but maybe we should."

"What bothers you?" I asked.

"For one thing, she kind of hopscotched around from country to country. Belgium, Egypt, Spain. That's kind of odd. I mean, people often go abroad in their own schools' overseas study programs, but she was hired directly by the universities in all these countries. Might be worth checking into."

"I'm on it," I said. I planned to see if my friend Paul Bickford could help me with researching the serious candidates. Of course, given his penchant for secrecy, I'd never reveal his role.

Crandell did not seem unduly disturbed by having someone who impressed him cast aside by Nunn.

"You two know more about this than I ever will," he said. "You might be right at that. We can't be too careful in our search. Too careful."

"Harrison Andrews Johnson. Let's talk about him," I said. The two of them pulled his file out and opened it. I let them read without saying anything. I was thinking about Duncan Delgado and Maxine March when Crandell spoke.

"I'll just jump in here, jump in here," he said. As he again repeated part of the sentence, Nunn looked at me, then winked.

"Very impressive, very impressive," continued Crandell. "He was an assistant Secretary of Transportation, an auto executive, and a highway commissioner. Those are high-powered posts. I think he might attract a lot of federal research money to the campus—the man has been there at the cusp of power, the cusp of power."

Nunn shook his head. He was not about to be intimidated by Crandell's fancy suit or his elegant conference room. "I'm afraid that kind of experience doesn't guarantee that he will know anything about running a large and complex university," said Nunn, "and the ability to obtain grants from the Department of Transportation won't do the sciences or arts much good, or agriculture and forestry, either. It won't amount to much, I'm afraid."

Crandell blinked a few times. I doubt anyone around these stately halls ever contradicted the senior partner of the firm quite so directly. I didn't say anything. Nunn was perfectly capable of speaking for himself. And, besides, I agreed with him.

"Well, I just thought his prestige might rub off on the university," said Crandell. "And he might have a rich wife. Didn't I see an aristocratic-sounding name somewhere in this file? Let's see. We'll just see." He began to shuffle the pages in the file. "Yes, yes. Here it is. My God, she's a Morgan! Now that is real money. And the right breeding and schools and social connections. Very top drawer, top drawer."

"I'm sorry to say that social position doesn't mean very much in Corvallis," I added. "Your campus title or your degrees probably mean more than your family connections."

"But, don't your faculty wives like to hold teas and things? I mean, have you no Junior League, no way for young ladies to come out?"

"I'm afraid 'coming out' has a whole different meaning on a college campus," said Nunn, barely stifling a smile.

"My God, I can't believe it, can't believe it!" continued Crandell. "Well, maybe I'm just behind the times. In my day at OU, things were more the way I described. Things were very different in my day."

It was time to bring the two of them back to reality.

"So, we can move Mr. Johnson onto the 'maybe' pile?"

"I'd like to toss him out right now," said Nunn. "Why waste our time with him?"

Crandell hesitated for a moment.

"Very well, then," he said eventually. "I bow to greater knowledge of the academic world. It all seems highly irregular, highly irregular."

"Let's move on to Joseph Henry Niles," I said.

"Another three names," said Nunn. "Maybe my name is all wrong. Two one-syllable names is pretty dull when you take it against this crowd."

Crandell and I smiled.

"Let's see. President of a small liberal arts college in Pennsylvania. Before that he was a dean there and before that a chair and faculty member in philosophy departments of three other colleges, all of them fairly small liberal arts institutions."

Crandell did not speak up like he did before, I suppose so as not to be contradicted by Nunn.

"Seems like a good enough background with progression up the ladder," said the oceanographer. "He's had administrative experience at many levels." He flipped through the file. "A good list of publications, too—both articles and books."

"What difference does that make insofar as his qualities of administration and leadership?" said Crandell.

"It means he's one of us," said Nunn. "He knows what we have to go through to get promoted and tenured."

"It's a very different system than you're used to, Mr. Crandell," I added.

"You can call me Alex."

"Thanks. Alex. It may be an odd system for doing those things, but we're stuck with it. No large national institution fights change more than higher education."

"That much I gathered," he said.

"He would bring to us a wife who is also a working academic," I continued. "Samantha Vicar-Niles is a chemist."

"Oh, I love hyphenates," said Nunn, a deadpan look on his face.

"Would that mean we'd get two for the price of one?" asked Crandell, hopefully.

"No, it would mean we'd have to offer her a position in the department of chemistry, whether there was an opening or not," continued Nunn. "When such a person is kind of forced on a department, the troops in the ranks don't like it very much. In fact, they could wind up hating her."

"But very quietly," I said. "She would be the proverbial eight-hundred-pound gorilla, the skunk at the picnic. But this can't be our concern now. If he's selected, the university and department would have to deal with it. We're looking for the best qualified person. Period."

"I'd say let's put him in the keeper pile," said Nunn. Crandell and I nodded our assent.

"Let's move right along to Joseph Svoboda."

They moved his file in front of their places and began to read. I thought to myself that things were moving along reasonably quickly.

"Mr. Svoboda is an engineer," I began. "He has jumped back and forth between working in his profession and teaching students about his profession. As you can see, he was a senior vice president of the big construction firm that did most of its work abroad building dams and air bases. Then he headed a big chemical company. A man of many parts. Seems like he comes in and saves companies."

"He, at least, has a good technical background," said Crandell. "I mean, he would be able to appreciate that part of the university's mission. Its mission."

"As long as he didn't turn out to be a philistine," added Nunn. "The arts and humanities have always taken second place to the technical and scientific programs. They get hind teat on the hog, if they get any teat at all!"

Crandell looked a bit uncomfortable at that remark, but didn't say anything.

"I agree," I said. "I've always been in the College of Liberal Arts, and we teach and work in the oldest buildings on campus. Our deans always have to fight harder for everything. But this isn't the place to air my personal feelings over budget allocations."

"I take your point, Tom," said Crandell, his voice sounding sympathetic. "I'll keep that in mind as I question our candidates. I really will keep it in mind. We have to train our students to be complete in their personas. As Descartes said, 'It is not enough to have a good mind but to use it well,' or something like that."

I liked what I was hearing. Crandell was not the befuddled patrician I had dismissed him as.

"I say we drop Svoboda into the pot and see how we like it when we get to know him better," said Nunn. Crandell and I nodded our agreement.

"Let's go to Lillian White next," I said. "She is pretty impressive. First in her class everywhere she went. First Black woman elected to the National Endowment for Humanities Board of Directors. She's taught and directed various arts and humanities centers on three campuses. She's a painter and a photographer. And, she's only forty-seven."

"What's the catch?" said Nunn. "Why is she coming here, to this White bastion? Compared to the circles she travels in, we're a backwater. A good reputation and a great place to work and live, but not for black people. She'd be cut off from her support system. She's single, so that could be hard for her to cope with."

"You don't think she's applying because of the challenges of the job and what she can bring to it?" asked Crandell.

"Not in a New York minute!" answered Nunn. "There's got to be something we don't know about."

"She is outstanding in every way, though," I said. "Want to propose her for a finalist, but ask lots of questions on her references? I'd hate to lose her at this early stage over something we don't know anything about."

"I agree," said Nunn. "Bring her in, but really dig in with the references."

"Yes, I concur," said Crandell.

"Want to question her references when we get to that stage, Chad?" I asked.

"Sure, why not? I'll give 'em the old third degree."

"So, I think our work is finished. We've gone through all the people our subcommittee was tasked to handle. Let's hope the other groups did as well. To recap what we did today: We put Lillian White, Joseph Henry Niles, and Joseph Svoboda on the 'yes' pile, Margo Baines on the 'maybe' pile, and Harrison Andrews Johnson on the 'no' pile."

"What about this other guy?" asked Nunn, holding up a folder.

I scrambled to find out who I had missed. "Sorry to misplace one," I said.

"Alexander Shay," said Crandell. "I must say, he looks like a president." He pulled a full-color photo of the candidate out of the pile and held it up for the rest of us.

"Yeah, so did Warren Harding," said Nunn, in his now familiar deadpan delivery. "But I shouldn't hold his looks against him."

"He's a psychologist and his experience runs the gamut from private practice to holding distinguished chairs at a couple of eastern colleges," I said. "Think he's worth a look?"

"I am impressed, very impressed with his vitae, and look at his letters of recommendation," said Crandell. "They're absolutely glowing. I think we would be doing a disservice to the university and our purpose here if we drop him at this stage of the game. A real disservice."

"I agree," I added. "I like the mix we have created: a humanities woman who is black, an engineer, a philosopher, and now a psychologist. What do you think, Chad?"

"I think he'd look great in his official photo in that conference room in the Memorial Union where all the presidential portraits hang. With that chiseled face and mane of hair, he looks like a million!"

With that, we adjourned.

The law offices of Lorenzo Madrid were in a rundown section of Salem, just east of the state capitol complex. There could not have been more of a contrast between the pristine elegance of Alex Crandell's palatial suite in a Portland skyscraper and Madrid's simple digs in a drab store-front building.

Five Hispanics were seated in the waiting room. When I opened the door, one of those little bells that stores use to announce customers tinkled loudly. As I walked up to a sliding glass window in front of the receptionist, a little boy looked from me to the bell and back again. When I winked at him, he buried his head in his mother's lap.

A pretty young woman looked up when I reach the partition and held up her hand. She was on the telephone.

"Yes, that is correct. Señor Madrid works for free. He is paid by the National Hispanic Defense Fund. There is no charge to you if he takes your case. Okay, then. You want to come in to see him? Tomorrow at eleven. Okay. But be on time. He has to be in court in the afternoon." As she hung up the phone, she turned to me and said, "How may I help you, sir?"

"I'm Tom Martindale. I called from Portland a few hours ago. Mr. Madrid said he'd squeeze me in."

"Oh, yes sir, he told me. Let me tell him you're here."

"I hate to go ahead of all these people." I gestured to the room. Mr. Fairness.

"It's okay. They are all very early. Some need our paralegal only—to take statements."

The five all smiled and nodded.

"Muchas gracias," I said to the group.

"Por nada," came a murmur from several people, including the little boy.

"All right then. I'm happy to see Mr. Madrid."

The young woman, whose name tag said Rosa, got up and walked to the rear of the room. Within seconds, Madrid bounded out of the back and motioned me through a door to the side of the reception area. *"Uno momento,"* he said to the group, holding up one finger. I hoped I'd have more time than that.

"Good to meet you, Mr. Martindale," he said when we reached his small office at the rear of the building. We had passed two smaller rooms on our way down the hall; inside, paralegals were taking the statements of people sitting across from them. "Sit down, please."

Madrid looked like the movie actor Andy Garcia. He was handsome, with fine features and skin the color of light brown sugar. Unlike the finely tailored suit he wore in court, today he was dressed in jeans and a work shirt.

"How can I help you? You mentioned my former client Hector Morales on the phone. He has flown the coop. That's all I know. A stupid thing to do. He'll get caught eventually, and it will be much harder for him. He's no angel. Hector is a gang-banger who has been in trouble with the law all of his life. I like to think that no one is beyond redemption, but maybe Hector is an exception to that little rule of mine. He's a bad apple, no question."

"But you took his case?"

"Everyone deserves a fair shake, their day in court," said Madrid, "even a gangbanger. He'd had a troubled life, but don't they all. But I need to talk to you about your interest in this. You were pretty vague on the phone." He smiled, but crossed his arms in a universally accepted body language sign that says, "I'm not telling you anything more unless you convince me I should."

This was no time for the deviousness I sometimes employed to find out what I wanted to find out. "I was in the jury panel for his trial."

"That's where I've seen you before. I couldn't place you. Now, I remember."

"You threw me off the jury."

"Oh, yeah, I guess I did. Don't take it personally. You are a former reporter, as I recall."

I nodded.

"I guess I had a wild hair up my ass about reporters that day. I worry about jurors doing too much investigating on their own. We attorneys don't like jurors doing any solo work beyond what we give them in court. I had the feeling that you like to look into things in just that way."

He had nailed me, no doubt.

"Am I right? Huh, huh?" His face broke into a big smile, his perfect teeth making a nice contrast against his skin.

"Well . . . I shouldn't . . ."

"I *am* right!" Then he began laughing. "Good that I nipped a bigfooter in the bud!"

"Yeah, I have been accused of worse, believe me! Anyway, I wondered if you knew anything about a guy you did select for the jury, Duncan Delgado."

"Hmmm. Not sure I remember him." Madrid stared into space for a while, as if he thought the answer would appear on his office wall, next to the Cesar Chavez poster. Then he said, "Yeah. I remember him now. Kinda flamboyant. Used to getting his way, I think. Seemed pretty full of himself."

"You picked him without asking him much of anything, as I recall."

"I hate to admit it to you, but I think I just picked him because he was a fellow Hispanic like Hector and me. Remember the redneck woman who called Hector a spic or greaser or some bad name like that? That's what we deal with all the time. I get it, and I'm well-dressed and well-educated and, I hope, well-spoken. If it happens to me, you can imagine how often it happens to guys like Hector Morales. I was just lowering the odds against it by putting a sympathetic guy on his jury."

"Do you know if he and Delgado knew one another?"

"God, I hope not. I could be disbarred if I permitted anyone on a jury who knew the defendant in any trial. Why do you ask?"

"There was a moment when Morales was first brought into court when he looked at Delgado and seemed afraid of him. It seemed to me that he was startled to see him there and did not like it."

"Hmmm. I wonder . . . but, I have no knowledge of anything like that. I'd never do that knowingly."

"I know you wouldn't, Mr. Madrid."

"Lorenzo, please."

"And I'm Tom."

"But what's your interest in this whole thing beyond whether they knew one another or not. That can't explain why you're here today."

"No, you're right." I decided to tell the truth as a way to get at anything he might be holding back. "Delgado's former wife is a student of mine."

"Okay, I get it. There had to be a woman involved." Madrid smiled broadly at his discovery.

"It's not what you think, at least at this point. She told me that she had met him during the sixties in Chicago, and they had both been involved in antiwar activities. He got a little rough now and then, and left her for a younger woman. She seemed scared of him—like Morales seemed scared of him. I just wondered if there was a connection. I'm not sure what I'll do with anything I learn. I just like to know what I'm dealing with if things progress between us."

"Perfectly understandable." Madrid opened the drawer behind him and pulled out a file. He started thumbing through it.

"Born in Chicago of Mexican parents, back to Mexico, then up here as an adult. Not sure why he moved to Portland." He read more. "Oh, my God! I can't believe it! How did I miss *that?*"

"What did you find?"

"Hector Morales listed Duncan Delgado as a personal reference when he applied for a green card. How the hell did I miss *that?*"

13

The fall term came and went fairly quickly. The search committee process ground on, with me doing much of the work. I made sure the other committee members did some of the references checking, but I was the one who provided the numbers and e-mail addresses and a list of questions.

By late into the winter term, we had honed in on five people: along with Niles, Svoboda, and White, we picked Ned Aliberto and Raymond Blandings. We put Baines, Johnson, and Shay on another list of decidedly low-ranking candidates. Things were going well.

I began to organize the campus visits of the finalists, set to begin early in May. That meant handling such things as airline reservations and tickets, transportation to campus, and housing. It also included planning the intricate minuet that we compelled the candidates to dance once they arrived in town. The exhausting routine included meetings with many of the university's publics, from faculty to students to alumni to influential public officials and media in the state.

Nancy Plumb helped me set up the series of lunches and dinners in public and private meetings. As we talked next to her desk, I noticed a photo of her husband, taken next to his stock car.

"How is Mike?"

"He helps me deal with all the pressures of my job," she smiled.

Hadley's assistant was always efficient; she even organized it all on a computer spreadsheet. Given my lack of computer savviness, I did not dare make even a small change in a schedule that included nothing but change.

"It's like herding snakes," she said at one point.

"Or cats," I laughed.

"I like the snake comparison better."

"Given some of the people we have to deal with, I guess you're right."

I spent my weekends on search committee matters. As I read the various dossiers, I made a note to contact Paul Bickford about looking into our finalists for anything that was nonpresidential and might embarrass the university. I jotted down subjects that popped into my head: business ties, intelligence connections, mental problems, family members with skeletons in the closet.

What else? I added: ties to the so-called military-industrial complex during Vietnam or more recent wars in the Middle East, like in Iraq.

✳   ✳   ✳

Last year, when I agreed to teach a course during the spring term, I hadn't known I'd be running a presidential search. But as I got more and more engulfed in the minutiae of that task, I decided the class would be a welcome diversion. To help a bit, though, my chairman agreed to let me limit enrollment. The small number of students who had signed up would make it easier still.

The course—magazine article writing—was one I had taught many times before. In fact, I could probably do it with my eyes closed. The trick was to not let my students know that. It wasn't fair to them for me to give my lectures on automatic pilot. Even though I knew the material well—by virtue of teaching the course for years and my own experience as a freelance writer—I shouldn't make it look that way.

As was my custom on the first day of class, I was in the room before the first student arrived so that I could greet each person and hand them a course outline.

"Good morning. Welcome to magazine writing."

A young man stopped in the middle of the doorway, looking confused.

"Er, I . . . isn't this Math 125? I really need it to get off probation. I'm still a freshman after two years here and I . . ."

"Afraid not," I interrupted. "Let me check the class schedule." Skimming quickly, I found his class. "Try Kidder 204. This is Stag 204. The building you want is across the library quad." I pointed vaguely to the east.

"Thanks, man. I mean, sir. Awesome!" On his way out, he nearly bumped into and knocked over a woman I knew well.

"Oh, my. Oh, dear. Please be more careful, young man."

"Watch your curlers, Granny," he grinned.

"Mrs. Meyers," I said, walking over to help steer her into the room. "How good to see you again. You're a glutton for punishment to take another course from me."

"You remember me, Professor Martindale. I *am* surprised."

Edna Ruth Meyers had taken a class of mine many years ago. Despite my early impression of her as a blue-haired lady without much talent, she had proven to be a better than average writer who was serious about her work. And she was still at it after all these years. She had to be in her eighties, but she looked no older than before.

"I never forget the good students," I said, handing her an outline.

"Oh, dear, I am so glad."

A tall, wiry man was next through the door. "Mr. Martindale, I'm Gary Hancock."

"Tom Martindale. Welcome to J417."

Hancock was probably in his early fifties, but the lines in his face and his sad eyes made him look older. He sat down and began to read the outline I handed him.

"Goll. Wow. Is this a writing class? I mean the one where you learn to sell stuff to magazines? I want to write for *Vogue* or *Glamour*."

I could always spot a sorority girl. Not only were they better dressed than the norm—designer clothes versus the usual indistinctive attire out of communist China in the days of Chairman Mao—they were also somewhat bewildered, often lacking street smarts.

"*Vogue* and *Glamour* might be right up your alley," I smiled. "Both are fine magazines."

The young woman smiled and seemed reassured. She took an outline and walked right to Mrs. Meyers, appearing to avoid Hancock's stare. His haggard face and full beard made him look as different as possible from the normal fraternity guy or jock she was used to spending time with. Hancock's eyes seemed to undress her as she flounced around him to a seat.

"J417?" A familiar Black kid came next—Ricky Lee Washington.

"You got it. Don't you get enough of me on the committee?" I laughed.

"I thought I'd see what all the fuss was about," he smiled. "I wanted to see if you're really a teacher."

"Fair enough. But the jury's still out on that. I didn't think you were interested in writing, Ricky."

"Everybody's got a story. Maybe you can teach me how to tell mine."

Maxine March walked in just behind Washington. I hadn't seen her since our odd encounter at the coast months before. I thought she had dropped her idea of taking my class or had even moved away.

"Ms. March."

I handed her an outline, and she moved to take a seat. She was wearing tight jeans and a somewhat skimpy tank top, a little too skimpy for her age. Hancock soon fixed on her, and she returned his unblinking stare without embarrassment. In fact, his stare not only failed to intimidate her, it seemed to act as a magnet. She sat next to him and made a great show of putting down her books and getting out a notebook and pen. I found this irritating, even though I had no reason in the world to be irritated at anything she did. I made a point of consulting my notes and my class list.

"I guess that's it. We're all here."

The members of the class glanced around as if they were confused.

"Way too few to keep this class goin'," said Washington. "Might as well pack up your stuff now and head for the registrar."

"Do we meet minimums?" asked Hancock.

"Oh, goll, I hope so," gushed the sorority girl, who I saw from the class list to be Penelope Soriano. "Like, I need this class for my communications sequence. What else will I add?" She seemed on the verge of tears.

"There, there, dear," said Mrs. Meyers. "Mr. Martindale is a kind man. He will take care of you." She reached over and patted the young woman on her cashmere sweater-clad shoulder.

"Penelope . . ."

"Pen. My friends call me Pen."

"Miss Soriano, Mrs. Meyers is right. I'm teaching this as an overload, so we don't have to reach the usual enrollment levels. And we can have the luxury of a small class."

"Awesome."

"All right."

"Great."

That would probably be the last time the class agreed on anything, but we were off to a good start. I would enjoy having a small class, too. It would allow for the good discussions you could never get with the twenty-five or thirty students that was the typical enrollment minimum.

"Good. I'm glad to hear you're pleased. Now, I usually spend the first day of class going over the course outline and requirements. Feel free to interrupt any time you have questions or comments. Let me say that I'm always available to talk to you. This term, though, I've got a lot of other responsibilities, so it'll be best if you make an appointment for during class."

"Mr. Martindale is very good to his students," said Mrs. Meyers, with a knowing nod of the head. "He's a kind, gentle person."

I was embarrassed by her flattery. "Maybe we'd better let them decide that after they get some graded assignments back," I laughed, in an attempt to shift the focus back to the class. "So, tell me what you want to get out of this course."

"The start of a memoir about my life as a teacher in a one-room schoolhouse in eastern Oregon," said Mrs. Meyers, with a smile at the memory of a happy time in her life.

"Say what?" said Washington, a look of disbelief on his face. "You had all the kids in one room, with you teaching all grades?"

"That's right, young man. I taught little guys . . ." she held her hand low ". . . and big ones." She raised it above her head.

"I've never heard of anything like that," said Washington, shaking his head. "Man, oh man. That's something!"

"Mr. Washington, how about you?"

"I'm thinking of writing about a fishing trip I took with my grandfather when I was ten. He and I really clicked, you know. Only way I could get away from where I lived in L.A., you know, the infamous Watts area."

His eyes glowed at the memory of what must have been a wonderful time in what I guessed was a sad childhood. But I had to spoil it.

"Mr. Washington, I hate to be the skunk at the picnic on this, but what you describe sounds more like an essay or even a short story. This is not a writing class of that kind."

"You sayin' we don't write stuff?" His eyes flashed. "What kind of bullshit is that?"

Edna Ruth Meyers looked as though she might collapse. "You shouldn't talk to the professor that way," she scolded.

I ignored what both had said. "Anyone, why is his story not journalism?"

"Because it's opinion and is just his personal view," said Penelope Soriano. "I mean it sounds sad and . . . and . . . interesting. Goll. Like, I'd read it!"

"What else?" I continued.

"There's a limited market for it as a piece of journalism?" said Maxine March.

"You're both right," I said. "What you propose is too narrow to be the kind of article we're going to write in this class. If you

broaden it out a bit, it would be fine. Let's say your grandfather's love of fishing, when he started fishing, where he came
from. Stuff like that."

"I can't find that out," said Washington, a sad look on his
face. "He was killed last year by a guy trying to steal his car."

"Oh dear, you poor boy," said Edna Ruth, reaching over to
pat Washington on the knee. He seemed to welcome the comforting tone and nodded gratefully to her, a tear in his eye.

"We're all sorry to hear that," I said.

"Why don't you broaden it out to cover how fishing helps
people in areas like Watts, I mean . . ." Hancock spoke for the
first time.

"Ghettos," said Washington. "It's okay to call it that, because
that's what it is. I'm here to get away from it, that's for sure!"

"Exactly," continued Hancock in a kind tone. "We're all here
to get away from something or someone. What I'm thinking is
you could talk to other people in your old neighborhood and
ask what they think about fishing. Did they fish when they
were kids, maybe in the South? Watts is a long way from the
mountains or a river, I'd guess. Or do they go to the ocean?
That's what I'd do."

I kept quiet and enjoyed what was taking place. In the ran-
dom selection of students for any class, teachers usually come
up with one of two results: a group who do not seem interested
and are unresponsive, or one where everything meshes from
day one. This one seemed to be in the latter category. Days like
this made me glad I was a teacher.

"You could still use your grandfather, but he would not be
the only source and subject," added Maxine.

"So Ricky," I said, "how's that sound?"

"It sounds great," he said, smiling for the first time. "I get it
now, I really do."

"Who else wants to talk about a subject?"

I glanced around the table. "Penelope?"

"Pen," she said. "Like, you can call me Pen."

"Sorry. You mentioned that. What are you planning?"

"Well, I was thinking I might write a history of my sorority, Gamma Gamma Delta. I really love being a member, and I love all the girls I'm in it with."

"Bore-ing!" muttered Maxine in a loud whisper.

"You care to say why, Ms. March?" I asked, as Soriano frowned and seemed on the verge of tears once again.

"I wouldn't read that. It seems pretty one-dimensional. I suppose the sorority magazine might use such a story, but they already know that sistership stuff. I may not look like it, but I was once in a sorority. Its tendency to exclude all but a select group of snooty girls really turned me off. I mean, if Ricky was female, would you let her—I mean him—in? I don't think so."

"We're not racist," said Soriano, her eyes flashing. "You can't know anything about us!"

I kept quiet to see how it would play out.

"I did not mean to imply that," countered Maxine. "How about something that reports on the downside of sorority life, as well as the rosy picture you seemed to want to paint?"

"I'd never do that! Like, I couldn't!"

"There, there, girls. Let Professor Martindale help resolve this."

I could always count on Edna Ruth Meyers to ask me for a Solomon-like decision.

"I'd agree with Ms. March to the extent that your first approach has a pretty limited market. When we talk about markets next week, you'll see that a freelance magazine writer has to look for the broadest audience possible. Think about who else might want to read your article beyond young ladies who are members."

Soriano nodded and stared out the window as if an idea might appear on the side of the next building or in the large spruce tree.

"That leaves the two of you. Ms. March and Mr. Hancock."

The two exchanged glances before he spoke.

"As you might have guessed by the way I look, I'm a Vietnam vet," he said. "I went over there when I was a kid and I came out a man, I guess you might say. I guess that sounds corny but it's true. I think I'll maybe compare my experiences and those of a few buddies with the kids who are coming back from Iraq. I'd bet they'd have similar things happening to them—I mean boy into man stuff."

The rest of us nodded in agreement.

"So, why is his story not objectionable like you all felt mine was," said Washington, not unkindly.

"Anyone?" I looked around the room.

"In the first place," said Maxine, "it sounds like he intends to interview people right off the bat. There doesn't sound like there'll be much opinion."

"Okay. Good. What else?"

"There's a definite tie-in to what's in the news," said Mrs. Meyers.

"Good," I added. "We call that a news peg. Something to hang your hat on, so to speak." Then, glancing at the clock, I realized it was time to wrap up our class discussion. "We're running out of time. What about you, Ms. March? What's your idea?"

"It has a Vietnam era theme, too. I was involved in the 1968 Democratic convention in Chicago. I got roughed up by the police, and it changed my life. I'd cover that and interview others I know who were there and how it changed them. There might be a tie-in to today, if I could talk to people who've been radicalized by the war in Iraq."

"Good approach," I said. "Our time is almost up. This has really been a good first session. You've helped each other out in bringing your ideas into focus. In the next class, I'll talk about how the magazine business is set up, and what the different markets are. Then, I'd like you all to take a stab at preparing a query letter about your article."

"Say what?" asked Washington.

"That's a letter to a magazine in which to present your idea in a paragraph, and tell who you are and give your credentials for doing such an article. No editor's going to offer you an assignment without knowing if you've got the background to do the job. Understood?"

All five of them nodded.

"The format is on page 56 of your text."

I held up the book open to the page in question.

"You'll need to consult *Writer's Market* for guidelines on what certain magazines are looking for. You don't want to send something on fishing, let's say, to a hunting magazine or one that is about classic cars. That would be a waste of your time and postage, and the editor receiving it would write you off as someone who didn't do his homework. Speaking of editors, pick a real person to address the query to. That means looking at the magazine. Unless the entry in *Writer's Market* tells you, you'll have to decide. If you start your letter by saying 'Dear Editor,' it'll get thrown away real fast."

"So, how long should this letter be?" asked Soriano.

"One page or two at the most. Anything else?"

No one said anything.

"Good. We'll read those queries in class next time. I'm looking forward to seeing what you do with your subjects."

The five of them packed up and drifted out the door. I busied myself with my own impedimenta. I was hoping

Maxine would stay behind for a private word, but she did not come forward.

"Want to get some coffee?" Hancock said to her. "Seems like our subjects have a lot in common. Who knows, maybe we have a lot in common."

"That's the best offer I've had in a long time," she said in a voice just loud enough for me to hear, as they walked out the door. I waited for them to leave before I made my own exit.

Why did I feel jealous? I had no right for any such reaction, but there it was, much to my consternation.

Joseph Henry Niles astounded everyone by knowing the names of all the committee members as he walked around the room, shaking hands.

"Now THAT is preparation," I whispered to Hadley as he got to me.

He was a short spark plug of a man who resembled the actor Ed Asner. His handshake was firm, and he looked me in the eye.

"Professor Martindale. I look forward to working with you."

He didn't pause for reply, but stepped to the next person in line, Gloria Gordon, the somewhat ditzy former alumni association president. She grabbed his hand and would not let go.

"Why, thank you, Dr. Niles," she gushed. "One seldom finds such courtesy in today's frantic world. I do really appreciate your knowing my name. I was president of the Alumni Association, and I can only imagine how pleasant it would be to work with you. I wish . . ."

"Move along, dear. You don't want to keep these busy people waiting."

I was startled to see the woman who had come into the room with him rise from her seat and, quite literally, pry Gloria's hand from that of her husband. Gloria frowned and sat down, her lips going into a pouty mode.

"My wife, Samantha, ladies and gentlemen," Niles said nervously. "She keeps me on task."

He stepped in front of Ricky Lee Washington, who quickly tried to "high five" him. Niles seemed befuddled and a bit frightened at this and tried again.

"Don't linger, my dear. Just move past this unfortunate creature."

Mrs. Niles was muttering through clenched teeth, but I heard what she said very clearly. So did Washington.

"What did you say to him?" His black eyes flashed, as he glared at both them.

"I was speaking to my husband, my boy. I was not speaking to you."

"Who you callin' boy, you skanky white bitch!"

Gloria Gordon seemed near collapse. "Oh, dear. I so hoped for civility."

She started fanning herself with some papers on the table in front of her. I looked at the chairman, hoping he would intervene, but he did nothing.

"Ricky, I'm sure Mrs. Niles meant no disrespect to you." I had reached his chair by now and put both hands on his shoulders, hoping to keep him in his chair. "Dr. Niles, this is Liz Stein from Political Science." I nodded at Liz, but kept the pressure on Ricky.

"Mrs. Niles, I wonder if you'd be more comfortable if you sat next to me at the table." Hadley had stepped in to help me. The tall and impeccably dressed woman immediately complied.

By this point, her husband had moved along to Chad Nunn.

"Oceanography has been an interest of mine since I first saw that French fellow on television." He looked at his wife for help.

"Jacques Cousteau," she mouthed the correct name.

"Yes, yes. Jack-ques Cantous. Very fine mind, very fine. I daresay that my love of the sea goes back to *Moby Dick* and Jules Verne. That giant squid gobbling up that underwater sea craft. Do you study squid here at Oregon University, professor?"

"No, I'm afraid not. No giant squid in our waters." Nunn looked amused, but he glanced at me and shook his head very slightly.

Niles had finished his round of handshakes by this time and was taking a seat next to Chekhov, the chairman, at the head of the table. His wife sat on his other side. As soon as he was settled, he drank from a bottle of water. He was perspiring slightly. At this point, his wife slid a stack of index cards in front of him. He squinted at them before she handed him a pair of glasses, which he put on.

Niles cleared his throat. "I am happy to be here on this fine campus on such a lovely day," he began. "It would be a wonderful . . ."

Chekhov touched him on the arm.

"Before you begin, Dr. Niles, I want to welcome you and Samantha to Oregon University. We trust your stay here will be a pleasant one."

Both man and wife smiled and nodded approvingly.

"I wanted to ask you to begin by telling us your impressions of our campus. It is a campus, I might add, that we are all very proud of."

Niles looked confused for a time, but then his wife reached over and pulled the proper card out of the stack, like a dealer in Las Vegas finding a hidden ace at the gaming tables.

I strained to see the heading. Appropriately enough, the words in capital letters were IMPRESSIONS OF YOUR CAMPUS. So much for the originality of our questions. I also began to wonder how many interviews Mr. and Mrs. Niles had been through.

It went on this way for over an hour, and I grew increasingly doubtful that he would make the final cut. If he had a note card containing the answer, Niles did fine. He was a good reader. If he could not find one, he would look imploringly at his wife, then smile at the rest of us, answering, "I'll have to get back to you on that one."

"Just like Ronald Reagan," I muttered, "without the acting experience."

*   *   *

Lillian White's skin was the color of light chocolate. She had a quick smile, but her eyes did not miss anything. They darted to each of our faces, as she shook Chekhov's hand and sat down next to him.

"We welcome you, Dr. White," he said. "We hope you are enjoying your stay with us."

"Finally a sister!" said Washington loudly.

"Some members are even more glad to see you than the rest of us are," said Chekhov to scattered laughter and applause. Gloria Gordon looked uneasy. Liz Stein did a clenched fist salute.

"I wondered if you had any kind of opening statement."

"Yes, Dr. Chekhov, I do. But first, I want to say how great it is to be back on your fine campus. I attended a summer workshop here more years ago than I care to remember."

Laughter and quiet mutters of approval issued from board members. They liked her and her easy banter was a nice contrast to Niles, who could not say "good morning" without consulting his cards or his haughty wife.

"This is a fine institution, one I would be proud to head. I can think of nothing more gratifying than looking out across the campus from the president's office. It would be a nice contrast to where I live now. Pittsburgh is not as beautiful as Corvallis or Oregon, for that matter."

White then began a concise analysis of the strengths and weaknesses of Oregon University. I was sure she had solutions for each problem, but she stopped short of giving them to us. She was waiting to cover that in her answers to our questions.

"We will begin our questions with Dr. Gomez, head of our new Hispanic Studies program.

"*Buenos días y bienvenido,* Senora White." Gomez smiled at White.

"This campus is not hostile to minorities, but it is not a place where you see many people of color. You live in Pittsburgh. I come from Chicago. Both of these cities are home to many people of color."

Chekhov shifted uneasily in his seat. I wondered where this discussion was going, but I welcomed it. Ethnicity and race were often submerged on campuses like ours without a record of attracting and keeping members of minorities either as faculty members or students.

"That's correct, Dr. Gomez," said White. "But I don't . . ."

"Forgive me, Senora, but I do have a point. You are a single lady?"

White nodded.

"Then you are going to be very lonely here."

"I don't see what Dr. White's private life has to do with . . ." interrupted Checkhov.

"Let the dude finish, professor," said Washington.

"You will have no support group to even socialize with. Up until a few years ago, there was, to my knowledge, only one

Black professor. Maybe a few more have been hired since . . . same for people from Hispanic backgrounds. Very few."

"Now, see here, Dr. Gomez, are you implying that we are a racist institution?" Alex Crandell was practically shouting. "As an alumnus of this fine institution, this fine institution, I resent that remark. I met my wife here and all three of our children have graduated from here. I don't like what you are saying. The very fact that we have asked Dr. White here as one of our finalists proves that we are not prejudiced. We are not prejudiced."

Crandell did not honestly know how condescending his last remark was. Liz Stein picked up on it immediately.

"You just reinforced your racism," she said, looking at Crandell. "Dr. White should not be invited to help our statistics. I mean, getting points for asking a Black person who is a woman. Double the score like in a card game. She should be asked because she is one of the best qualified candidates to become our president."

"That dude is a racist and a dumb shit to boot!"

"Ricky, I will have to ask you to leave the room if you use profanity," shouted Chekhov, who was rapidly losing control of the meeting.

"I wonder if we need a coffee break," I said to break the tension.

"Yes, Professor Martindale," chimed in Hadley, "that's a great idea."

Many members of the committee got up and left the room quickly, Washington in the lead. When the door opened, a young man from the catering department wheeled in a cart containing drinks and cookies. Lillian White had stayed in her seat. She smiled when I handed her a glass of iced tea and an oatmeal cookie.

"Good grief, I really caused a little firestorm," she said, shaking her head and taking a bite of the cookie.

"Ricky was probably born a hot head," I laughed, "but some of what Dr. Gomez said is true. This is a very white town. It is hard for me to put myself in his shoes, but it must get pretty lonely. The university has always tried to make people of color feel welcome, but not everyone in town gets the memo. There have been incidents from time to time."

"I make it a point to ignore incidents. There are stupid people in all shapes, sizes—and colors," she said. "I'm a big-picture girl." She smiled broadly, but there was sadness in her eyes. "It wouldn't be easy to turn this place around, but I'd give it my best shot."

Before I could answer and let my neutrality slip, the other members of the committee began coming back into the room. Most made their way to the refreshment cart, a few sat right down.

"I think we need to bring this session to a conclusion," I whispered to Hadley.

"Don't I know it," she said. "Dimitri's so upset he left the building. He's got high blood pressure, you know. I'm going to take the chair slot."

She turned to the others.

"If we could take our seats quickly. Dr. White has a session with the Faculty Senate leadership in another building in thirty minutes. We need to make sure we keep her on schedule."

The others took their seats rapidly.

"Good. You're all being very obedient."

Hadley's easy way with people and generally calm demeanor brought the atmosphere in the room back to normal. The drinks and cookies helped, too.

"I think you will all agree that this is neither the time nor the place to talk about the racial climate on campus or in this city. Dr. White is our guest, and we owe her the courtesy of hearing her closing remarks. Unless anyone objects, I'd like to move to that phase of our meeting now."

No one at the table disagreed.

"Dr. White."

Lillian White stood up and faced the committee.

"I believe in higher education for everyone, no matter the color of his or her skin. That has been my mission in life since I knew enough to have a mission in life."

She paused and looked around the room, engaging the eyes of every committee member.

"If I am lucky enough to be chosen president of this fine university, I will try to make sure that we do not wear race on our sleeves—or as a chip on our shoulders."

She glanced at Ricky Washington, and he quickly looked away.

"We will make this place a haven for all those who want to better themselves by working hard to learn—how to be good thinkers, and how to be good people. Questions of race will be cast aside, as we strive to reach that higher goal."

She stopped and drank some tea.

"My personal goal, if I am chosen as your president, is not to be Lillian White, the first Black president of Oregon University, but Lillian White, the new president—who happens to be Black and a lady."

She sat down and munched calmly on a cookie.

After going to a movie on Saturday night, I drove downtown to have a cup of coffee at Starbuck's. As I turned the corner onto Madison Street to look for a place to park, I saw Maxine and Delgado sitting at one of the sidewalk tables. They seemed to be arguing.

As I slowed the car and glanced over to where they were sitting, she got up and started to walk away. He reached for her arm, but she pulled away. I rolled down my window to call out to her.

"Leave me alone, Duncan! I'm warning you! If you keep screwing around with my money, I'll tell the university what I know about you, and your precious ass will be in a sling."

"Threats do not become a beautiful woman like you," he said mockingly. "Come home with me so we can talk about another fine ass—yours!"

"*That* will be the day!"

I rolled up my window and drove away. In the mirror, I could see her walking up the street in the opposite direction, then turning the corner onto Fourth Street. I drove around the block and saw her again. A car pulled up and she got in. As I passed it, I glanced at the driver. It was Gary Hancock.

* * *

Seeing Maxine, first with Delgado, and then with Hancock, reignited my curiosity about all of them. That night, I called my Special Ops friend Paul Bickford at home.

"Hi, Paul. Are you in some kind of deep cover or can you surface long enough to talk to a mere mortal like me?"

"You are so full of shit, Martindale," he laughed. "I was just sitting here eating match heads for their high sulfur content. Keeps the mosquitoes away, you know."

Although he was kidding, I knew Bickford well enough to wonder if that was exactly what he was doing. Guys in his line of work often did odd things just for the fun of it. They weren't called "snake eaters" for nothing.

"I've got someone else for you to check out, Paul."

"Another presidential candidate? How much dirt do you need on these people?"

"We've already got so much to hold against them, we'll never have a president," I laughed. "Actually, what you got me really helped. Thanks again. This request is more of a personal one. I need some information on a student." On the spot, I decided not to press my luck by asking for more information on Delgado. I'd just see what he could find on Hancock.

"And why is that? You know, it's against federal law to pry into the affairs of American citizens that aren't a threat to the country. This person doing some minor-league anarchy out there, Tom?"

"No, I wouldn't call it that. He's a Vietnam vet, I think."

"When did that become a crime?"

Bickford was really putting me through my paces here. But I had to admit that I was stretching the facts in talking about Gary Hancock. I wanted Bickford to find out something bad about him so I could tell Maxine. And why, pray tell, would I do that?

"Okay, okay. It's personal. There's this woman in class who . . ."

"Bad to go after the coeds, Tom. That's getting into moral turpitude territory. That's what you call it, isn't that right?"

"She's not a conventional eighteen-year-old. She's my age, and I like her—a lot."

"And the Vietnam vet is horning in? So you want to impress her by telling her bad stuff about him so she'll like you better."

It sounded ridiculous and pathetic and underhanded, but he was right.

"Yeah, I guess you might say so, Paul. You've always been able to guess my motives."

He chuckled. "That's why I'm such a good spy. I wouldn't do this if we weren't good friends. Now, what's his name?"

* * *

Two days later, I was in my office grading papers when my phone rang.

"Tom Martindale."

"It's Bickford, Tom. Are you alone?"

"Yes, Paul. Any luck with Hancock?"

"More information than you may want to hear. He's got a past. He's not exactly a nut case, but he's been carrying on a kind of one-man crusade against chemical companies since his time in 'Nam. Blames them for making the herbicides used there to defoliate the jungle."

"Yeah, yeah. He talked about being a Vietnam vet in class. Go on."

"He first came onto our radar in the 1980s, when he began writing letters to congressmen and senators. He was respectful in tone, but asked for compensation for our troops who had been exposed to Agent Orange."

"You mean those doing the spraying got sprayed too?" I asked.

"Oh, yeah. It happened all the time. If the people supervising the spraying miscalculated on things like weather or wind direction, all that bad stuff could blow right back onto them."

"Sure. It makes sense that that could happen."

"Also, troops on the ground sometimes got sprayed, either by the same kind of drift or because of mistakes. At the time, the Defense Department disputed a G.A.O. report about the health problems of people serving there. It said that American troops did not enter sprayed areas until six weeks after the defoliation. The G.A.O. found at least 5,900 Marines were within one-third of a mile of the sprayed area during and shortly after defoliation missions and that another 16,100 Marines were within the same proximity four weeks after spraying."

"Just like now," I said. "The government always denies the obvious."

"The official 'me' has no comment," said Bickford. "The 'me' that's a rational human being agrees with you."

"So, what happened to these guys?"

"You name it, they've got it. All kinds of cancers, birth defects in their children, rare and painful skin diseases," he continued.

"Hancock looks healthy enough, but you never know," I said. "Maybe he's sick in the head. I mean, if he's been obsessed with the issue for so long."

"He continued to write letters to members of Congress for ten years or so, then he escalated his activities."

"How so?" I asked.

"First, he picketed, and he's suspected in some mysterious fires at a plant. Then, he threatened some bigwigs at one of the companies—or may have threatened them. It's kind of murky. Authorities could never pin anything on him. As far as we're concerned, he dropped off the radar for a few years, but since I've just heard that General Chang is coming to your campus in a few weeks for commencement and security will be a top priority for me, maybe I'd better take a look at him."

"I hate to get him into trouble," I said.

"I'll have it done discreetly, Tom. It could be nothing. It could be a matter of national security. We won't know until we check it out."

"What's the company he targeted?"

"Let's see." I could hear Bickford shuffling through papers. "Lone Star Chemical Company, one of the smaller manufacturers of herbicides. They were forced out of business after an impurity was found in their process. The Forest Service sprayed some of their stuff to clear brush in a forest someplace in Arizona in the 1980s—some kid got leukemia and died, and a higher than normal number of miscarriages took place. A lot of the people sued and won, and it put good old Lone Star out of business."

As he talked, I was shuffling through my own papers. I soon found what I wanted.

"Paul, one of our candidates for president was president of Lone Star in the 1980s."

"I think I'll be seeing you sooner rather than later, Tom."

I heard a dial tone in my ear. Paul Bickford had hung up.

* * *

On Sunday, I drove by Maxine March's apartment building on my way to dinner. My resolve toward my normal policy of not dating female students of any age was gradually weakening. Even though she was about my age, it was still a bad idea to see her socially outside of class. Much to my dismay, I found myself being drawn to her, both physically and intellectually. I had to see her—now.

As I drove around the corner, I saw her get out of a car about a half block from her building. I slowed down and double-parked. As she got out of one side, someone else got out of the other.

Gary Hancock grabbed her around the waist and pulled her to him. She kissed him passionately, then they walked toward the entrance to her building. I waited until they went inside before driving away—quickly.

There was plenty of discussion among the committee members about Ned Aliberto long before he arrived on campus. A last minute addition, he had not been as carefully considered as the other candidates. I guess we had a fear of the unknown, but we invited him anyway to broaden the pool of applicants. His letter accepting our invitation to the interview contained several unusual requests. For example, he wanted to know the dimensions of the public rooms of the president's house and even the capacity of the water heater. I turned those questions over to the director of physical plant and promptly forgot about them.

Unfortunately for me, Dr. Aliberto did not.

"Which one is Martindale?" he asked, as soon as he arrived in the conference room.

"That would be me," I said, walking over to him and extending my hand.

He ignored my offer to shake and started gesturing. As with some tall men, he used his height—about 6′ 4″—to try to intimidate me.

"Did you not get my requests for information on the house? I thought I had worded them very simply."

For an idiot like me to understand, I thought to myself.

The people in the room stopped talking to listen to my response. I'm afraid it came out a bit sputtery.

"Yes, you did, Dr. Aliberto. I turned your requests over to the people who take care of the house, but I did not follow up— I'll admit it. I will get on it before you leave campus today."

"See that you do," he replied icily. "I must say, I don't like buck-passing by people who work for me. I don't like excuses, either. I want action!" He seemed to grow another inch or so, as he straightened his shoulders to loom over me even now.

"In the first place, sir, I do not work for you. However, I will do my best to get those answers, short of going out to the house with a tape measure."

Ah, the magical protection that comes with tenure.

"What department did you say you are with, Professor Martin, was it?"

What a shit, I thought to myself.

"It's Martin*dale*. From the journalism department."

The ever-resourceful Hadley saved the situation from deteriorating further. "Dr. Aliberto," she said, as she gently nudged him into place at the head of the table, "I think we'd like to get started if you are ready."

Aliberto grunted and followed her lead. I decided to sit farther down the table than usual. I wanted to get as far away as possible from this man I already knew I couldn't vote for.

"We have begun each of our sessions with candidates with a round of questions from our members. In keeping with our rotation format, the first question goes to Dr. Chad Nunn from oceanography; Dr. Nunn holds a distinguished chair in marine geology, and he came to us from the Woods Hole Oceanographic Institute in Massachusetts."

Aliberto seemed bored with everything Hadley was saying. "Whatever," he said, with a wave of his hand.

I had never seen such a display of indifference and arrogance. He was, after all, asking us to recommend him for a job.

"Good morning, Dr. Aliberto, and welcome to our campus. I hope you have the chance to see some of its beauty and are not kept inside meeting rooms for your entire time with us."

"I thought you had some questions for me," Aliberto said abruptly, as he started tapping a pencil on the edge of the table.

"You got a train to catch?" muttered Washington in a loud whisper.

"Ricky, please," said Hadley.

"I mean, the dude's impatient. We all got places to be!"

Aliberto glared at the young man, but said nothing.

"I wanted to ask you about one aspect of your plan to improve the university," said Nunn.

"And that would be . . ." More pencil tapping.

"Your desire to triple the president's entertainment budget and to totally remodel the president's residence. And what is this about the purchase of a plane?"

"I come from the private sector," said Aliberto, with a look of incredulity on his face. "Large companies treat their executives well. The feeling, I think, is one of tending to creature comforts so the man in charge feels happy and contented and has the desire to work even harder."

"But in a university, we . . ."

"I have not finished, Dr. Noon is it?"

"Nunn."

"Forgive me. Dr. Nunn. I have also headed several small, private colleges. They were heavily endowed, and we had generous allowances for travel and entertaining. "

"But did you have your own plane?" I asked.

"Am I to answer two people at once?" he said to Hadley, completely ignoring Nunn and me.

"Sorry, Dr. Aliberto. Just deal with Dr. Nunn's question now," she replied.

"As I was saying before the interruption,"—frowning at me—"a plane would make better use of my time when I visited other states to bring in the funds you so desperately need." He nodded in agreement with his statement. He seemed to be having a dialogue with himself and no one else.

Nunn pressed on.

"What about the increase in the budget for entertaining? It is already at $50,000."

"I think the food served at the president's table needs to be of the highest quality. Outside caterers are a must—from Portland, perhaps? We simply must have the best in Oregon wines, as well. I'm not sure about you, Dr. Nunn, but I fancy myself somewhat of a wine connoisseur. I think the mark of a man's sophistication are the wines served at his table."

I could not believe how out of touch Aliberto was. With all the problems the university was facing, the quality of wines served at dinner was way down my list. The others were also looking a bit dazed at the exchanges. Getting nowhere with this line of questioning, Nunn moved on.

"There is also the matter of the president's house. I have only been up there on a few occasions, but it seemed to me to be quite nice." He opened a folder and pulled out several pages. "The state bought it a little over five years ago. It has, let's see, a large living room, a dining room that seats twenty, and four bedrooms with private baths." He turned to the next page. "I see there is also a separate building with two offices and an area for a secretary or assistant to work. Did you not see the house or photos of it?"

Nunn looked at Aliberto, who smiled and shrugged his shoulders.

"I did get a cursory tour of the house, but did not get the actual room measurements. At a glance, it did not seem like it would adequately accommodate the guests I would be inviting. And the kitchen is very inadequate. I would need to examine the dishwasher, refrigerator, and hot water heater to see if they could handle things . . ."

"Those parties sound elegant," said Gloria Gordon, batting her eyes at Aliberto. "If you need any help in co-hosting, I'm your girl. I've got many sorority sisters who would pitch in to help, I just know they would."

"My dear lady," said Aliberto. "I will certainly keep that in mind."

I was certain that having Gloria anywhere near an event put on by the Alibertos would never happen.

"Could we agree to defer further discussion of the house until a final decision is made," said Nunn. "It's very premature at this point."

"With one caveat," said Aliberto. "I was leading up to a major point: without many changes and some costly remodeling, the current building is not suitable to house the president of the university. I would ask that an agreement be prepared to the effect that any job offer to me includes the stipulation that a new house will be built within two years of my taking office."

"And that is something that is nonnegotiable?" asked Hadley.

Aliberto stood up before he answered. "Yes, it is."

"Then I guess we must reluctantly decline to consider your candidacy any further. Thank you for coming and have a pleasant trip home."

With that, Hadley walked out of the room. Many members quickly followed, leaving Aliberto virtually alone at the table. I stayed behind to help him pack up his things. At first he would not look at me. Finally, he spoke.

"I have seldom been treated this shabbily," he shouted. "I will not be shy about expressing my displeasure to any colleagues who ask. This is a backwater university and will never dig its way out of its trench of mediocrity."

I was determined not to rise to the bait and give him something else to complain about.

"I am sorry you feel that way," I said, showing concern that I did not feel. "I will see that you get a ride to your hotel."

Saying that, I walked out of the conference room, leaving the clueless Aliberto to wonder why things went wrong.

In class later that day, it was time to read the final articles aloud, as a way to get feedback from the other members of the class and me. The helpful "me" was happy to tell students how to outwit the grading "me" that would be holding the red pen in a few weeks. I always enjoyed this point in the regular term because it allowed me to see if students had grasped any of the concepts I had been trying to teach them. I was also curious to discover if any of the men and women in the class had real writing talent—I mean ability beyond what it took to get an "A" from me.

I was not sure I could help the students all that much. I was preoccupied with running the president search and more personal matters, like Maxine March, Gary Hancock, and the mysterious Duncan Delgado. I couldn't seem to take my mind off any of them—separately or together. Needless to say, I was disgusted with myself.

Maxine chose to read parts of her article first.

"Here goes nothing," she said to the rest of us. "I might as well get this over with. It's a personal story, but once I was part of a major event that became a turning point in my life."

She looked good as she arranged the pages and started to speak. She had deemed this an important enough occasion to dress up a bit, her usual proletarian attire replaced by a yellow turtleneck and black cords. She had even put on a necklace.

I lived all my life in Chicago in the neighborhood that Al Capone once called home. It was a fairly conventional life until one day in August 1968 when I went with my room-mate at the University of Illinois to what was going on at the Democratic National Convention.

For several weeks on campus, Wednesday, August 28, had been talked about as the big day. The demonstrations against the Vietnam War were expected to reach a crescendo that night. Organizers of the protests hoped to entice at least some of the television cameras into the streets outside the hall where a candidate was being nominated.

Signs proclaiming "the whole world is watching" were everywhere that day. Later, the huge crowds would turn that sentiment into a chant that they shouted for hours.

I hitched a ride with my friend Rose to Grant Park. By this time, there were thousands of people milling around. Despite their collective hatred of the war, the crowd had an almost festive air. Some people danced and sang in impromptu performances. Others made love amid the general chaos. There was a lot of nudity and pot smoking.

Just as it was getting dark, the crowd started walking out of the park toward the hotels that lined it on one side. We all knew that many of the delegates and some of the leading candidates, like Humphrey and McCarthy, were staying in those hotels. Even if we looked like a ragtag army of anarchists as we headed out, we were far from that. Interspersed here and there in our midst were young men and women with walkie-talkies trying to keep us orderly. Many were veterans of the civil rights marches in the South, so they knew a thing or two about crowd control.

As we walked, we kept up the chant. "The whole world is watching." And indeed, it was, because by this time we had been joined by several television crews. I can only describe my feelings then as giddy. I was having fun, and dumb and innocent as I was, thinking that my presence was going to make a difference.

After about ten minutes or so, I sensed a change in the crowd ahead of me. They suddenly got very quiet. It took a few seconds for those of us in the middle ranks to figure out that something had changed up ahead. The chanting drifted off into the humid night air, then ceased altogether.

"Oh God, no!" An older man ahead of me, who was a bit taller than those around him, saw them first.

I strained to see, but could not.

"Jesus! What are they going to do?"

Now it was an older woman just one row ahead of me who had a clear view.

"What is it?" shouted people around me.

"It's the pigs," said a gaunt young man with a peace sign painted on his forehead. They're going to get us!"

On we went, keeping our ranks fairly well intact. I had no compulsion to run away or dart to the side for safety.

As I heard the first cries of anguish from those in the front ranks, that line from a Lit class I took the term before came into my head. It was from Tennyson's The Charge of the Light Brigade—"Into the valley of death rode the six hundred."

Along with the human cries, I began to hear the thump of police batons against the skulls of the marchers ahead. Then, the police shot tear gas at us. When this happens, you don't really see anything. But before you know it, you just can't breathe. As you are gasping for breath, you can't think of anything except getting fresh air into your lungs. The euphoria I felt at being a part of something big and something good evaporated in an instant.

My only thought was that I had to get out of there. People were running in all directions. I joined them, dragging Rose along with me. We climbed over a wall and got away. The only thing that happened to me was a scraped knee. I think I was lucky.

Maxine stopped reading and looked up. "Kind of intense. I guess. Sorry if I depressed you."

I looked at the others. Edna Ruth and Penelope were crying. Gary looked grim. Ricky was the first to speak.

"She-it! I thought only Black people were under the heel of the man. Good stuff. Riveting."

"Oh, my dear, how you suffered," said Edna Ruth, reaching over to pat Maxine on the arm.

"It took a lot for you to put that on paper, I know it did," sniffed Penelope. "I admire you so much. Goll, like I don't think I could ever write anything that personal. It was awesome!"

"How do you plan to broaden out your story? I mean, to put it into the perspective of the whole antiwar movement?" I asked, eager to get everyone settled down. "And what's your market?"

"I guess I didn't get that far," she said. "I thought maybe my experience would be powerful enough on its own."

"It is powerful enough," said Gary Hancock, giving me a dirty look. "Anyone who thinks otherwise is just plain wrong!"

*   *   *

The next day, Hancock read his work. He hadn't said all that much during class or stayed afterwards as many quiet students do to have a personal word with the professor without anyone else overhearing. I was curious about how he would handle the subject in his article.

The other students seemed just as interested. All of them sat in rapt attention as he shuffled his pages in preparation. He put on wire-rimmed glasses and looked around the table. He put a cough drop in his mouth and cleared his throat.

"I'm kind of hoarse today. I think I slept in a draft."

He looked at Maxine, and she returned his smile. It was clear to me that they were sleeping together. I suddenly felt flush and wiped my brow. I was angry at the thought. I had no right to care who was the object of her affections. It made me mad at myself to give the subject a second thought.

"This is another story about the Vietnam War. Ms. March lived through that turmoil on the home front. I served over there when I was still a kid."

I found myself calculating Hancock's age. 55? 53? He was in great shape for a guy of that age. Trim, slightly muscular, a full head of hair. Only his face betrayed what he had been through. About my age—and Maxine's. But, I needed to concentrate on what he was saying.

"So here goes." He cleared his throat again and began to read.

I hadn't wanted to have anything to do with defoliation and the chemicals that brought it about, but when you're in the military, you usually don't have a choice about what you wind up doing. It seemed like an okay job at first, and I was too young to weigh the consequences.

Defoliation was a program used by the United States government in Vietnam for most of the years we fought there in which chemical herbicides were sprayed over wide areas of the countryside to strip plant cover from areas occupied by Vietcong and North Vietnamese forces and to destroy crops that might provide them food. By the time I got there, the chemicals had been used on 5,000 square miles of South Vietnamese territory. The whole country totaled 66,350 square miles. By one estimate, a million acres were sprayed each year.

The U.S. government justified the spraying as a military necessity. After a while, people living next to the sprayed areas began to report illnesses they blamed on the chemicals. Adults and children became ill. There was a greater percentage of miscarriages at the Tudu maternity hospital in Saigon than before the spraying began. There were also a higher number of birth defects among the children who survived than in the past, such as stunted growth and learning difficulties.

As usual when it makes such a mistake, the United States government denied that any kind of harm had resulted from anything it had done. Because its intentions were stellar, it was above reproach.

Even after an American C-123, flying out of the Bien Hoa Air Base on December 1, 1968, developed engine trouble and dumped its full load of defoliants on two small villages, the government discounted any problems. Residents of Tan Hiep and Binh Tri northeast of the air base were subjected to all the chemicals on the plane within thirty seconds. Normally, the spraying lasted over four minutes at a rate of three gallons per acre. The air would disburse the herbicides over a wider area, presumably one where no people were living.

The defoliant was a fifty/fifty mixture of 2,4-D and 2,4,5-T. Both of these chemical compounds were used in weed killer products sold over-the-counter at garden stores all over this country and overseas. Over time, warning labels and better packaging were mandated and some uses banned.

After this emergency dump, no physicians visited the two villages to examine the people after their exposure. And, like eight similar emergencies, this one was not made public by the United States command in Vietnam. A U.S. Air Force medical team visited the area right after the spraying and, predictably, found no one suffering ill effects. There was no later inquiry.

A New York Times reporter visited Tan Hiep a year later and interviewed a woman who was convinced that her youngest son—who the reporter said looked like a newborn child even though he was fourteen months old— had health problems because she breathed chemicals on the day of the drop.

Her neighbors blamed the spraying for the fact that their children—one a year old, the other ten months old—were still unable to walk. Both pregnant mothers had been working outside on that day.

A farmer in nearby Binh Tri had told reporters that two people died three days later from respiratory problems and trembling. At their funerals, the people of the villages blamed the deaths on the spraying.

With the war going badly over the next few years, the problem gradually got swept aside. Damage to people and animals in sprayed areas became the least of the U.S. government's problems.

Consistently, official statements about the spraying over the seven years it went on played down the harm and played up the good it did to thwart enemy movement and conceal-ment. A 1966 report by the U.S. State Department described the sprayed area as "remote and thinly populated." It went on to note that the chemicals sprayed on the vegeta-tion were less potent. "The herbicides used are nontoxic and not dangerous to man or animal life," read the report. "The land is not affected for future use."

What was left out of such comforting reassurances was that the original research on the defoliation chemicals and other herbicides occurred during World War II. That research considered them for use in military programs in bio-logical warfare. A scientist who advised Secretary of War Henry Stimson on such matters was quoted in a New Yorker article about the intended usage: "Only the rapid ending of the war prevented field trials in an active theater of synthetic agents that would, without injury to human or animal life, affect growing crops and make them useless."

After the war, the same herbicidal materials were put to their current weed-killing use. The testing for military use was continued at the U.S. Army's Fort Detrick facility in Maryland. When the need arose in Vietnam, the products were ready. They were combined into a product called Agent Orange, the color designation coming from the stripes gird-ing their shipping drums. (There were also an Agent Purple, an Agent White, and an Agent Blue. Agent Orange is the compound whose name survived, mostly because of its wide-spread use.)

This is where I come into the picture. I was an eight-een-year-old Air Force grunt in 1970, trained to do what I was told. What I was trained to do in that year was to open spigots of death that let these harmful herbicides rain down on the innocent men, women, and children below. Inadvertently, I became their killer in much the same way as if I had fired my gun at them or stuck them with my bayonet.

Hancock stopped reading and looked up. He took off his glasses and began to cry. Both Maxine March and Edna Ruth Meyers, sitting on opposite sides of him, patted him on the arm.

"It's late," I said. "Why don't we resume this reading on Monday." I gathered up my materials and walked out the door. I would leave the comforting to others.

＊　＊　＊

That night as I was watching the news on television, the telephone rang.

"I was prepared to talk to your voice mail message."

"Hello, Paul. How are things in the world of super sleuths?"

"As always, I won't rise to the bait or even dignify your comment by a response."

"I'm sorry, Paul. I admire what you do, really. I only kid the people I like."

"What I'm about to tell you didn't come from me. In fact, it didn't come from anyone. It kind of drifted into your head from someplace in space."

"I hear some buzzing in my head right now. What do you have?"

"I dug up some interesting stuff on your friend Duncan Delgado. He's kind of a slippery character without much of a paper trail, so I had to go a couple of layers down to get what little I got."

"I'm not surprised. He's kind of spooky."

"He's had a number of important benefactors throughout his career. Nearly all of his research has been funded on the first try, both from public and private sources. That is, until recently."

"Yes?"

"Last year, his request for a full-fledged study of the effects of the Ebola/Marburg virus was turned down. He had gotten funding for preliminary work in the same area for the past five years."

"So what was different?"

"That's what is interesting and maybe disturbing. Before, he used conventional laboratory animals in his work, mostly monkeys. This time, he wanted to use human subjects."

O ther than the nuclear reactor, the Animal Isolation Laboratory was the only building on campus that had access restricted to the small number of people working there. The one-story, cement block building was surrounded by three rings of chain-link fences topped with razor wire.

The security precautions were the result of two concerns: keeping any fumes and toxins caused by the work in the lab from getting out and causing harm, and keeping animal rights protesters and terrorists from getting inside to sabotage the work by releasing animals or stealing live viruses.

In order to find out more about Duncan Delgado's work on Ebola/Marburg, I concocted a need to interview Malcolm Mandelbaum, the lab's director. That ruse would get me in the door, and I'd figure out my next moves as I went along.

In preparation for the interview, I did a lot of background research on the subject. What I discovered was pretty scary.

Since the Ebola virus was first discovered in 1976 at a remote jungle mission in Zaire, its potential lethality had worried scientists worldwide. The virus is named for the river where it first appeared.

On August 28, 1976, a thirty-year-old man came to the Yambuku Mission Hospital complaining of terrible diarrhea. After two days of treatment, the man left the hospital, just as sick with diarrhea and a severe nosebleed, never to be seen again. Within days, more people came down with the same symptoms. A week later, people began to die horrible deaths.

As reported by a government doctor on the scene, Ebola fever is "characterized by high temperature, frequent vomiting of black, digested blood, but red blood in a few cases; diarrheal emissions initially sprinkled with blood, with only red blood seen near death; epistaxis (nosebleeds) now and then; retrosternal and abdominal pain and a state of stupor; prostration with heaviness in the joints; rapid evolution toward death after a period of about three days, from a state of general health."

Nine years before, three workers at a vaccine-producing laboratory in Marburg, Germany, had come down with similar symptoms. In the next few weeks, twenty-three patients were near death at the Marburg University hospital. Then a veterinarian and his wife came down with the disease in Yugoslavia. By December 1960, seven of the patients had died; all had bled to death with blood pouring out of all body openings. Some patients survived, but were left with permanent liver damage leading to chronic hepatitis. A few developed psychiatric problems.

The World Health Organization conducted an investigation to find a cause for the disease. Where had they gotten this new viral hemorrhagic disease? They soon found the answer: all of the original cases in Germany and Yugoslavia involved men who worked with monkeys. More specifically, all had handled animals, or the tissue of animals, from Uganda, and all the monkeys came from three shipments of wild animals transported from just over the border from Uganda to Belgrade, Yugoslavia, then to Marburg and Frankfurt.

When the first shipment arrived in Belgrade, 49 of 99 monkeys were dead. The survivors were placed in quarantine under the care of the veterinarian who later got the disease. He had autopsied the dead animals.

In the years since the two viruses first appeared, new outbreaks of both Ebola and Marburg have occurred in Africa. Scientists think the two are closely related, causing hemorrhagic fevers that can be fatal within a week. Death rates run as high as 80 or 90 percent. In Angola, in 2005, 340 of 408 victims died.

There is no vaccine or treatment for either disease. In early 2005, however, scientists in both the U.S. and Canada reported success with a new type of vaccine that prevented the disease in monkeys. They said it was the first step toward producing human vaccines. The new vaccines, one for Ebola and one for Marburg, were 100-percent effective in a study of twelve monkeys. They would not be ready to be tested on people for two years.

The research had broader implications, according to what I read. Not only would the vaccines stop outbreaks of Ebola and Marburg, it might also protect people from germ warfare. This aspect of the research had brought me to the office building inside the first ring of fences where Mandelbaum had his office.

A secretary looked up as I walked in the door. She quickly brought up her screensaver to hide whatever she had been working on.

"You're Professor Martindale," she smiled. "We don't get many visitors out here."

"I doubt many people know you are where you are. I expected some kind of security," I said, gesturing out toward the fence.

"All the fences can be electrified instantly. We've got security guards roaming around at night. Any intruder would be arrested—if he didn't get zapped first. Dr. Mandelbaum is expecting you."

She got up and walked to the closed door behind her desk. She knocked on it, then opened it, disappearing inside. She emerged in a few minutes carrying some papers and a large binder.

"You can go in."

I did just that. Mandelbaum was tall and slender.

"Excuse me for not getting up," he said, before extending his hand. "I broke my foot rock-climbing three weeks ago, and the damn thing didn't heal properly. That's why I had you come out here. I usually don't see visitors in this office because of security worries, but it was just too much of a hassle to go onto campus. Once I'm ensconced behind my desk, I try to stay put. I had you checked out, though. You seem pretty harmless to me."

"That's what my former girlfriends say—and my students," I laughed.

"You are researching an article on our work here relative to finding a vaccine to treat both the Ebola and Marburg viruses?"

"Yes, for the *Smithsonian* magazine. I'm doing interviews with some Army researchers at Fort Detrick, too."

"Impressive. Will you get to Africa?"

"I doubt it. I don't have a travel budget."

"Just as well. There isn't much going on in the way of research in any of the countries with major outbreaks. Zaire, or the Democratic Republic of the Congo as it is now known, barely functions as a country anymore after that tyrant Mobutu got through looting it. Angola is very poor, too. There's no money to help people who suffer from the diseases, let alone pay for research into what causes them. Also, you wouldn't want to risk coming down with the disease yourself. They're both very bad diseases; people die horrible deaths when they get either one. Look at these shots."

Mandelbaum pulled some photos from an envelope and slid them across the desk to me.

"Are the readers of the *Smithsonian* ready to look at this over their white wine and goat cheese?"

The men and women in the photos had blood oozing out of their mouth, ears, and eyes. Their skin was covered with a crimson rash. I had seen graphic photos of dead and dying people in my years as a reporter, but these made me gag.

"Have some water," he said, filling a glass from a carafe on his desk. "Happens to the best of us. I'd worry if you didn't feel sick to your stomach. It's a very ghastly virus."

"Before we get into your findings, can we talk about the national security aspects of the story?"

"Only a little. We are constrained by Army security rules. In fact, I'm going to be a bit vague at times about what we are finding because I don't want to tip off our enemies."

He drank from his own bottle of water.

"Our security concerns date back to the 1990s when a Soviet defector said that the Russians had stockpiled the Marburg virus, weaponized it, and packed it into warheads for possible attacks on cities or battlefields. Although Ebola and Marburg used in such attacks would not be as lethal as, say, smallpox, they could kill a lot of people or leave those who lived with impaired health. This is not to mention the huge economic burden of caring for them."

"The Russians are our allies now. Is the threat over?"

"On the contrary, what's to prevent a crazy person from selling the makings of the virus to an Arab terrorist group, or even from turning a bunch of infected monkeys loose in Grand Central Station in New York City? I think it's simply a matter of time before this happens in a large metropolitan area. Future outbreaks may not be in a jungle."

Mandelbaum looked at his watch. "Sorry, but I'm late for some physical therapy on my foot. I've got time for maybe one more question."

"You bet. How does the vaccine work?"

"The vaccines are made by using another virus, VSV, which causes a mouth disease in cattle but rarely infects people. It has a similar genetic structure to the Ebola and Marburg viruses. Other researchers have also had success with it in developing vaccines. They altered VSV by removing one of its genes, thus making it harmless. Then, they replaced it with the gene from either the Marburg or Ebola virus. The transplanted gene forced VSV to produce Marburg or Ebola proteins on its surface. The proteins can't cause illness, but they provoke an immune response that protects the animals. Researchers at Fort Detrick watched the monkeys for signs of illness after they were injected with Marburg and Ebola."

"Do you use monkeys here?"

"I'm not going to tell you if we are conducting experiments on live animals here. I don't want to give the animal rights radicals any excuse to attack us. Let me just say two things: we don't use monkeys in our research, and there are other ways to conduct testing without using laboratory animals."

"You mean, with people?"

"I can't answer that except to say such experiments are rarely allowed. These viruses are very dangerous. A Russian scientist died in 2004 at a former Soviet biological weapons laboratory in Siberia after she accidentally stuck herself with a needle laced with Ebola. That same year, an American scientist at Fort Detrick had a similar accident, but did not die. It's extremely dangerous."

Mandelbaum struggled to his feet and reached for his crutches. "I've got to get going, if I ever want to walk properly again."

We shook hands.

"Thanks for your time. I'd like to call you later if I have questions."

"Sure, sure. You can also call Duncan Delgado, my second-in-command. He knows everything I know.

We walked to the door, he hobbling along on his crutches, me bringing up the rear.

"I've met Dr. Delgado," I said, not all that anxious to cross paths with my erstwhile fellow juror. "I will call him if I need anything more."

✳ ✳ ✳

That night, I put on dark clothing and drove to a parking lot near the university theater where I left my car. Then I walked west toward the cow and sheep barns. Soon I reached the covered bridge that had been moved to campus a number of years ago to save it from destruction.

I shuddered as I walked across it, recalling an incident several years ago when I had found a body hanging from a support beam. As always happens, that led to my further involvement in solving the crime of who had killed this victim—an academic adviser in the athletic department—and also one of my own students.

My footsteps reverberated on the wooden floor of the bridge as I began my newest snooping adventure. One of these days, my curiosity was going to get me into real trouble—no doubt about it.

For the next mile or so, the terrain was fairly flat, except for berms along both sides of the road that were covered with tall trees. The campus was filled with wonderful plants and trees, many of them old. Their age made them tall, thick with foliage, and great to hide behind.

I could see the floodlights illuminating the lab before I saw the lab itself; when I could see it, I knelt down behind a small hill to observe the scene. I wasn't really sure what I was looking for, other than another piece of the puzzle that Duncan Delgado had become in my mind.

Did I want to get something on him to help Maxine? And why did I want to help Maxine? To get her into bed? To keep her out of a potentially dangerous situation? My motives were murky, but here I was, so I huddled down just to watch for a while.

* * *

I had dozed off when I heard the noise of a motor, then the clanking of the gate as it rolled open to admit a vehicle. As a panel truck drove through the gate, it suddenly stopped. The engine had stalled.

The driver got out and raised the hood. He was soon joined by the security guard who had opened the gate. Their preoccupation with the engine gave me my chance to sneak in. Crouching as low as I could, I ran down the small hill and across the darkened field to a point at the edge of the fence.

"Damned if I know," the driver was saying. "I only drive these things, I don't repair 'em."

"My dad could make anything run," said the guard, "but he didn't pass any of that on to me."

"We gotta get this baby inside and unload our cargo, pronto," said the driver. "It's pretty perishable. I don't want anything to happen to 'em."

"I'd better call it in," said the guard.

"Help me push it first." The driver was getting irritated.

"Jesus Christ! What's the hurry? It's only a bunch of animals. I'm callin' it in."

When the driver followed the guard into the building, I saw my chance and took it. Keeping the truck between the two of them and my line of sight, I walked into the enclosed area, ducking into the shadows not far from the door.

"You don't seem to realize what's going on here," the driver was saying. "I've got to unload my cargo."

"Okay, okay," said the guard. "I'll help you push it. I guess I shouldn't have left the gate open so long."

"You got *that* right," said the driver. "Delgado will have both of our asses if we screw this up."

After the driver got back into the truck, put it into neutral, and released the emergency brake, the two men walked to the rear and started to push. I stepped out of the shadows and ran through the open door.

The room was small and contained a large bank of television monitors mounted on the rear wall above a counter. The monitors showed what were apparently views of different parts of the lab. With little time to linger here, I headed through a door at the side of the desk.

"Son of a bitch!" said one of the men trying to push the truck. "This baby does not want to budge."

I closed the door behind me and stopped in the hall to check out my surroundings. The passageway seemed to run the length of the building with a number of closed doors lining its sides. I walked along the hall quickly, glancing into the windows on each door as I passed them.

The first two rooms on each side were empty. The third and fourth rooms contained cages, however. In the dim light, I could barely make out dark forms in each one.

"Let sleeping monkeys lie," I muttered to myself, pressing on.

More empty labs were to my left and right, as I continued down the hallway; the room on the left at the end of the hall was an office, containing two desks. I stepped in and opened a file drawer. Inside were folders containing papers with handwritten notes. The pages were headed "Research Subject #50M," "Research Subject #35F," and so on. The data meant nothing to me, so I quickly put the pages back and closed the drawer quietly.

Back out in the hallway, opposite the office was an intersecting hall; at the end was a door marked "Duncan Delgado, Ph.D., Associate Director." Inside was a small waiting room cut in half by a counter, where his secretary presumably sat.

I was surprised to find Delgado's door unlocked. His office was large, but fairly Spartan—he probably had another one on the main campus where he saw students and spent his public time. Having more than one office is a real sign of status on most campuses. I have often thought that the university did this in lieu of giving professors higher pay.

Three of the walls were lined with floor to ceiling bookshelves. The fourth wall contained a window and a number of framed photos and what appeared to be awards. I didn't bother to read them, but concentrated on the desk—or tried to.

Locked. Where would a cautious man like Delgado keep a key? Would he carry one with him without a spare? I looked through the items on the desktop; the phone, pencil holder, and IN box held nothing. Nor did the top of the credenza behind the desk. I got down on my knees and started looking under things—the chair, the one drawer of the credenza. Nothing.

Then I spied a key taped to the back of the printer next to the computer. I pulled it loose and peeled off the tape. It slid into the lock on the middle drawer of his desk, and I pulled it open—too quickly. The contents—pens, paper clips, staples, empty notebooks—clattered noisily.

I paused to listen for the footsteps of anyone who might have heard me. No sound, so I relaxed again. At the back of the drawer, I noticed a small box. Inside it, I found another key and a tiny card.

> *To Whom It May Concern: In the event of my disappearance, use this key to unlock the door to my private file room. Entrance behind right bookcase. Middle sections pull out to reveal.*
> D.D.

I walked to the bookshelves and pulled on them. They opened out like the double doors of a closet. In the wall behind the shelves was a narrow door held in place by a heavy padlock. When I inserted the key, the lock snapped open. I pulled on the door, and it opened to reveal a small room lined with filing cabinets. I closed the outer doors.

All of the cabinets were locked, of course. As I stood there imagining what the files contained, I saw a trapdoor in the floor at the far end of the room. I walked over to it and pulled on the ring gently. The door creaked as it came up.

The smell of human sweat and urine wafted up from below, plus disinfectant that did not quite mask the unpleasant odors. Down inside the hole was a steep wooden ladder; I could not make out the bottom rung in the darkness below.

Turning around, I stepped gingerly on the top rung and pulled the trapdoor closed as I turned on a small flashlight I always carry for my night excursions. I started downward, being careful not to fall.

Because I was going slowly, it took more than a minute to reach the bottom. Once there, I checked the floor before I stepped on it and discovered it was packed dirt. The tunnel opened up into a small room with a tall, maybe ten foot ceiling. I opened the only door out of the room and found myself looking down a long passageway lined, as luck would have it, with more doors. None of these had windows, so I had to open them. As I did so, I worried about what might be inside.

Fortunately, the first two were empty—of people or animals, that is. They did contain two rows of five cots each, all neatly made up with sheets, blankets, and pillows.

"Pretty classy accommodation for monkeys," I muttered.

What was going on here? Why did the research laboratory need places for people to sleep? I certainly haven't seen any people here—and only a few animals upstairs. I stepped back into the hall and walked on.

As I tried to figure out what I was seeing here, I heard voices at the other end of the hall. The driver and the guard were finally unloading their cargo, and it sounded like they were going to bring the poor monkeys down here by another ladder at the other end of the passageway. I did not envy them having to balance crates as they descended on a ladder.

I opened the nearest door and slipped quickly inside. Because there was no window, I would have to gauge the approach of the men by their voices or their shadows, which I could barely make out under the door.

My concentration on the men distracted me from my surroundings. By the odor in the air, I could tell that I was not alone in the room, and I could hear breathing and movement. The hair on the back of my neck stood up, and I got a cold chill. This had happened to me all my life when I was really scared of something.

More breathing and shuffling.

I eased away from the door and felt along the wall until I found the corner of the room. I did not feel confident enough to walk straight ahead for fear of what I would encounter. But, as my grandmother would say, curiosity killed the cat. I couldn't stand not knowing who or what I was sharing the room with. I snapped on my flashlight and shone it around. What I saw made me start gagging immediately.

The room was filled with cages stacked one upon the other, and the cages were filled with monkeys—some seemingly well, some sick, presumably with Ebola because blood ran from their eyes and noses.

"Oh God," I said aloud. "You poor guys."

I was drawn closer than I should have gone to several end cages. The eyes of a few monkeys looked at me so beseechingly I had to turn away. Other monkeys looked mean, and who could blame them?

I was so caught up in my feelings of revulsion that I did not see a particularly large monkey reach through the bars as I passed. He grabbed my arm in a grip as strong as a man's. As I struggled to get free of him, he started screaming. The earsplitting sound bounced off the metal cages and the walls so loudly that I thought my head would burst.

Luckily the monkey was weak from the virus and couldn't sustain that grip for very long. I easily pulled free of his fingers after several seconds. But he kept screaming.

By this time, the driver and the guard were in the passageway. Soon they would be outside the door. I moved to the wall next to the door and waited. If they did not open it too wide, the door itself would conceal me. If they came inside, they would find me.

As the monkey kept up his piercing wail, I started to sweat. There was no way to explain my presence here and no way to get away. I was outnumbered and outpowered; their brawn would easily overwhelm any superior mental ability I could muster.

I waited and the monkey screamed on.

"You hear that?" The driver, whose voice was deeper than that of the guard. "What the fuck is that? It's scaring the shit out of me!"

"Never mind. You're better off not knowing anything that goes on down here." The guard. "Just step back and let me look in."

I held my breath as the door swung open and bounced off my foot. Fortunately he paid no attention to that little maneuver. Some people have no curiosity. Then the guard turned on the lights, but did not enter the room.

"Shut up, you big cocksucker," he shouted to the screaming monkey. "Jesus, God. Why do they keep you all alive!"

The pitiful monkeys looked back at him as if they agreed. Even the big monkey grew silent.

The guard slammed the door, and I started to breathe again. I decided to stay where I was until I could figure out how to get away. Even the stench and the danger of infection were better than getting caught.

The sounds of the men's footsteps retreated to the far end of the passageway. I opened the door slightly and peered out. I could see up the hall to where the bottom of the ladder rested on the floor. The guard and the driver were looking up.

Surely, the new monkey "subjects" were not going to walk down the ladder on their own. Monkeys are smart but not *that* smart!

The first person to step off the ladder was a young Hispanic woman who looked scared to death. She was followed by a slightly older man carrying a little boy. The guard motioned for them to go down the hall toward where I was hiding. I eased the door closed and listened to them walking by. I guessed there were no more than ten, given the size of the van they came in.

"Andale, andale!" yelled the guard.

The foot shuffling intensified.

After ten minutes or so, things got quiet again. I could hear the muffled voices of the two men as they got their charges settled in for the night. *"Silencio. Buenas noches,"* said the guard.

The door closed and the two men walked past the door and down the hall. I waited until I heard them climbing up the ladder and the trapdoor above it slammed. Then I counted another ten minutes before venturing out into the passageway again. Although I was tempted to go into the room to see if I could help the people inside, I knew I could not—at least not at this point. I had to get help.

As I crept past the door, it opened suddenly and the little boy jumped out. I put my finger to my lips in what I hoped was the universal sign to keep quiet. Unfortunately, he ignored me.

"Mama, mama," he cried, as I stood there.

19

I scrambled up the ladder as fast as I could, losing my footing at one point so that I banged a shin. I ignored the immediate pain from what was probably a bad bruise—I didn't have time to look at my leg. Once up on the main floor, I closed the trapdoor and quickly got out of the building. Despite all the commotion that had erupted below, all was calm up above.

Maybe Delgado had disengaged the alarm system in order to keep university security people away. He probably ran everything out here, especially since his boss, Mandelbaum, was incapacitated with his broken leg. For whatever reason, I was glad that no alarms sounded.

As I walked out of the building, lights from a car skittered on the wall above me. I ducked down behind a hedge, then slowly made my way in a crouching position to a small building near the inner security fence. Luckily, the gate was still open.

The car halted next to the van that I had seen earlier. The headlights went out, and the driver's door opened. At first I couldn't see who the driver was, but when he walked to the other side, however, Duncan Delgado was visible in the head-lights. No one got out of the passenger side, even though he had opened the door.

"*Andale, por favor,*" said Delgado.

In a rapid-fire stream of Spanish I couldn't understand, he was trying to get someone in the car to come out. After a few minutes, he lost his patience; he reached into the car and seemed to be pulling on an arm.

Delgado's strength easily overwhelmed the other person, and he emerged quickly into the glare of the floodlights. Hector Morales put his hands over his eyes, then blinked when Delgado tugged on both his arms. He stood at least a head taller than Morales, who had not looked so small while sitting in the courtroom.

In another stream of Spanish, this time in a more stern tone than before, I could make out to the words *coyote* and *dinero*. I wondered if Delgado had somehow coerced Morales into act-ing as the procurer of this poor band of illegals—if that's what they were—and presumably engineering his release from jail so Morales could do so. Delgado's cunning, audacity, and resourcefulness boggled my mind.

How he had done this on the campus itself was beyond my comprehension. Why he had done this was easier to fathom. He wanted the glory connected to the scientist who discovered a cure for the Ebola virus, even if it meant trying it on human subjects. Or, he wanted the research dollars that come with the search, never mind the illegality and immorality of how he was going about it.

Delgado grabbed Morales's arm and pulled him toward the door. At that moment, the guard and the driver emerged from the building. The two put out their hands to shake with Delgado, but he ignored them. Instead, he started berating them in an intimidating manner. I moved slowly to my previous vantage point behind the bush so I could hear what he was saying.

"If I ever get even a whiff of any of this from anyone, you two are dead meat," he said. "I'm not paying you to open your mouths to anyone—and I mean, anyone. I know where you live and who your families are. I know you want them to be safe so you can enjoy the money I'm paying you. If you don't fuck with me, I won't fuck with you!"

The two nodded obediently and shuffled their feet.

"When . . . er . . . a . . . are we gonna get . . . um . . . a . . . our money?"

Delgado grabbed the guard by the front of his jacket and pulled him close. "Don't be so greedy, you little pissant!" he said in a loud whisper. "I'm going to give it to you when I'm convinced I can trust you." Delgado released the man, who almost fell down as he pulled away from the hulking scientist.

"Okay, that's better."

The other two relaxed a bit as Delgado reached into the pocket of his coat and pulled out two envelopes.

"Don't bother to count this now. You two need to get out of here. It's all there—a thousand dollars in small bills to go with the other thousand I gave you last month."

The two nodded and started to move away from him. He grabbed them by their arms yet again.

"Don't forget what I said about your families. Now, get out of my sight!"

Delgado turned his attention back to Morales. "We've got business to attend to, *mi amigo.*"

They disappeared into the building. I disappeared into the night.

* * *

Shortly after 4 P.M. the next day, a team of tactical officers from the Oregon State Police and the U.S. Immigration Service surrounded the Animal Isolation Lab. They gained admittance to the inner yard when the guard on duty saw their credentials and the size of their force.

I had called Angela at home the night before and then gone over to her apartment to tell her what I had found out. As in situations like this in the past, she was very skeptical of my story. Our relationship—sometime lovers, still close friends—finally caused her to act. I hadn't let her down in the past and that fact prevailed in the end.

She had put the lab under surveillance at dawn, and then it had taken all morning to assemble this team. Her lookout reported no suspicious activity. In fact, all had been quiet until the small staff arrived for work at about 8 A.M. Delgado himself had gone inside, but Mandelbaum had not, according to the officers on duty, who were watching from the same grove of trees across the road where I had hidden the night before.

Against what she called "her better judgment," Angela had let me ride with her to the lab; she always felt that way when I got involved in my amateur crime solving. I could usually win her over to my way of thinking, however. This time, my argument was that she would not have known about the illegal aliens without me. After a lot of arguing throughout the night, she had reluctantly agreed.

She made me promise to remain in the car throughout the raid. I readily agreed because I was after justice, but would just as soon keep my involvement secret. Even if he was under arrest, I feared for my safety if Delgado found out about my involvement. It could also have repercussions for Maxine, especially if he somehow found out about our friendship.

As I watched through the binoculars, the raid seemed to go smoothly. The teams disappeared inside the building. Soon after, the staff walked outside, all of them looking bewildered and a bit scared. I recognize Mandelbaum's secretary when she emerged. It was ten minutes before Delgado came out behind Angela, who was looking a bit over-dressed in flak jacket and helmet.

As seemed usual with him, he was gesturing wildly and arguing. They were too far away for me to hear anything other than loud voices. She was shaking her head and pointing at the papers in her hand, presumably a search warrant. Delgado was having none of it. Although clearly outnumbered, he was standing his ground.

In a few minutes, five men came out of the building. Their flak-jacketed leader walked over to Angela and whispered in her ear. She seemed dejected at what he told her. Their search had clearly come up empty-handed.

I got out of the car to get a better view of Delgado's reaction. He seemed to be smiling at yet another victory. As I took in the scene, a ray of sunlight caught the lens of the binoculars, creating a flash that attracted his attention. Although I hurried back into the car, he had clearly seen that someone had been observing. I doubted he could see that it was me; however, the incident made me nervous. I had seen enough of Delgado's ruthlessness to fear his reactions.

Raymond Blandings had been dean of science for ten years. With a mediocre record in that job, he was a surprise candidate for president and had not been on our first lists. Most search processes unearth an insider—often added for reason of sentiment, not competence—and a few get the job. But I doubted that Ray would be one of them. Under him, the College of Science had stagnated. Enrollment had declined and its few top researchers and teachers had left or were planning to leave.

That said, Blandings was a good politician. As he entered, he immediately put those talents on display. With his wavy gray hair and square jaw, his was the face you might see in fashion magazines in ads for clothing designed for older men. Rumor had it that he was also a ladies man, bedding secretaries and new assistant professors left and right. Twice divorced, Blandings played the field relentlessly.

"Dimitri, my old friend, I see they went for wisdom and knowledge when they picked the chairman of this august committee."

Chekhov looked a bit uneasy at Blandings's man-to-man embrace and pat on the back.

"My dear Vice President Collins. You look for all the world like you should still be in graduate school." Hadley winked at me as Blandings bent down to kiss her hand.

"Dr. Martindale, I presume." He started laughing at his own lame joke. "I hope that when the bodies start piling up, mine won't be among them."

He did not embrace me, but did pat me on the back heartily as he laughed a bit too loudly. Other people around us, however, did not join in the merriment.

"Gloria Gordon sent her daughter to today's meeting, I just know it."

The former Alumni Association president and sorority girl nearly swooned. "Oh, Raymond, it's SO good to see you."

Blandings kissed her wrinkled neck and whispered something I could not hear, and then out loud, "It can't be you, Ms. Gordon. You look fabulous!"

"She-it," muttered Ricky Lee Washington. "This cat's really full of it."

Blandings ignored him as he continued to overwhelm the fawning Gloria. "I remember an alumni board meeting in the Columbia Gorge." Gloria's face got red as she brought the memory into focus. "Oh noooo!!! You can't mention that!"

Then they both started laughing so hard the elderly Ms. Gordon had to sit down and fan herself back into recovery.

"Young Mr. Washington," the candidate said, as he tried to high-five the very hip Ricky Lee. The latter refused to give him more than a firm handshake. Looking befuddled that his attempt at brotherhood had failed, Blandings moved on.

"You are so tiny, Miss Chen. Like, may I say, a China doll."

"This cat's really out to lunch," muttered Washington.

"Tiny, but mighty," said Victoria. "I want to ask you what plans you have for scholarships for people of color."

"In good time, my dear," he replied. "I have a seven-point plan."

Blandings left Victoria Chen rather quickly; apparently the student's question was a bit more than he was prepared to answer at the moment.

"Alex, I'm so glad to see you again. I played golf with your senior partner, Andrew Binder, last week. Wonderful man."

"Yes, Ray, a wonderful man, wonderful man," said Crandell. He has time for golf, now that he's semi-retired. We working stiffs have to put in a full day, a full day."

"I . . . er . . . a . . . I was in Portland to meet with some visiting scientists from the Ukraine. Great to see you, Alex."

"Miss Stein, I . . ."

"It's Ms.," replied the usually confrontational political science professor. "I want to know how you feel about expanding the Women's Center and sponsoring a gay and lesbian collective."

"I . . . er . . . collective?"

"It would get university funding and a building and full-time staff to counsel students with ambivalent feelings about their sexuality and probably needs more AIDS awareness classes and a full-time nurse practitioner and, I guess, drug and alcohol rehabilitation. Many of our students are into drugs, and I don't mean to say that it's only gays and lesbians, but they're people too, even if not everyone agrees. Last year, I was in the Netherlands, and saw how they pay attention and care for young people in need. Not as much as in the Scandinavian countries, but good, nevertheless. The year before I was in Cuba, which has a superior health care system, including care for drug addicts and alcoholics. Not gays and lesbians, though, because Castro is very antigay and antilesbian. It is too much of a threat to his manhood or something, but when he dies all bets are off. But we can have good care for every student, gay or straight, but the gay ones need it more than the straight ones . . . so what do you think?"

Blandings had been blinking his eyes rapidly, almost in time with Liz's litany of problems to be solved, one blink per problem.

"Well, my dear, I . . ."

"I am not anyone's 'dear.' I am Liz or Professor Stein or Dr. Stein. When anyone calls me 'dear'. . ." she paused and shivered, "I get angry. It brings to mind all the men over the years who have been condescending to women and people of color and all the downtrodden."

"Professor Stein, I cannot possibly respond to all of your demands at this time. I do have a four-point plan for student enrichment. Maybe some of those people fall into those categories."

"They should not be called 'those people.' They are human beings. They are not faces in the crowd who can be expected to pay their ever-increasing tuition rates and get nothing in return."

Liz's eyes were flashing. These issues were very serious to her, and Blandings was not getting the message.

"I think we need to save Dr. Blandings's responses to specific topics for our next round of questions," said Hadley. "Maybe you should take your seat, and we can get to that now."

Blandings seemed happy for the rescue from the swamp of his own loquaciousness. He walked to the front and sat down between Hadley and Dimitri Chekhov.

The chairman seemed reluctant to fulfill his role. Throughout the interviews he had let others keep the committee members on track. "Very well, then, I think we need to . . ." He looked at Hadley, who reached across Blandings with the agenda for the day.

Chekhov looked at it as if he was seeing it for the first time. "Oh, yes, questions are next. Some of our members are so eager to have the benefit of your thinking, Dr. Blandings, that they already brought up a few matters. Let's start over here at my left, since you did not get to personally greet the people sitting there."

"Delighted, my dear Dimitri. Delighted!"

"Dr. Nunn."

"Dr. Blandings, I'm not sure we've ever met, so it is good to put a face to the name. I wondered about your thoughts on increasing university support for hard science. In oceanography, we have had to raise our own funds for years, even for people who teach part-time. We think that there should be a higher level of funding for people in those positions. What do you think?"

Blandings blinked and said nothing for a minute or so, as if he were searching a computer memory for the correct answer.

"I have a ten-point plan for increasing research funds. I'm a scientist, Dr. Nunn, so I know what you're thinking. As a former president often said—I mean a U.S. president, not president of this university—I feel your pain."

"When might we see this plan?" asked Nunn. "I'd be eager to share it with my colleagues in the college."

"I . . . er . . . a . . . it's not quite finished yet. My transition team is working on it right now."

"You have a transition team?" I said. "That seems quite premature to me."

"I can't say I like your tone, sir," said Blandings, his face reddening. "I thought it would be easier to get a running start on handling the problems I would face when I take . . . I mean, if I take this job."

"Or if it's offered to you," said Liz Stein.

"This cat's truly screwed in the head," added Washington, being no help as usual.

Blandings did not reply, but continued to straighten the pile of papers in front of him. From where I sat, they were only committee documents he had been given when he walked in, not a compendium of his plans to solve the university's present and future problems.

"I wonder if this is a good stopping point," said the ever-perceptive Hadley, as Chekhov stared out the windows to the south at the low-lying buildings that house the university maintenance shops.

As the committee members filed out, no one took the time to say anything to Blandings or engage him in any way. He sat at the table looking expectantly, his chiseled face contorted into a look combining disappointment and grief.

* * *

From the moment Joseph Svoboda entered the conference room, he seemed like someone who was used to giving orders—and having them followed to the letter. He was easily the best dressed of all the candidates, wearing a light gray pin-striped suit, a pale yellow shirt, and a yellow and red figured tie. His cuffs protruded equidistance from his suit coat, held together with silver cuff links. I don't think I'd ever seen anyone wearing cuff links in Corvallis during my entire twenty years living here.

Svoboda walked to the center of the head of the table and shook hands with Dimitri and Hadley before sitting down in the chair between them. I was so caught up in observing his attire that I did not see the woman who came in with him. That is, until the first time he snapped his fingers, and she handed him several sheets of paper.

She was dressed as plainly as he was smartly, in a dark non-descript suit that caused her to blend into the background of most rooms she entered. Her graying hair was fashioned into a bun at the back. Her shoes were what my grandmother called "old lady shoes," except that she did not appear to be as old as I. She would not have been bad-looking with a little makeup. I'm not saying that she would have had a magical transformation, but she would look a lot better than she did now.

Svoboda, who looked about sixty, was trim and looked fit, probably the result of many hours with a personal trainer—who probably was not summoned by a snap of the fingers.

"Ladies and gentlemen of the committee, I am pleased to introduce our last candidate for president. Joseph Svoboda has been head of the Office of Technology for the Department of Energy and a member of the board of the National Endowment for the Humanities. Earlier in his career, he was president of the Matthews Group, a consulting firm. He is now a private consultant to governmental industry in Washington, D.C. Mr. Svoboda."

"It's *Doctor* Svoboda, actually," he said without smiling. Snap!

His assistant, whom he did not introduce, turned on his PowerPoint presentation. Our attention was directed to the first panel of it.

"My vision for Ory-gone University is to create a shining castle on a hill to which federal and private grant money would begin to flow to expand our research here."

"Excuse me, excuse me." I said. "Our first priority has, and I hope always will be, undergraduate education. Graduate education is important and funding for research is vital, but we still focus on undergraduates. That's why I'm here, and I suspect many of the people around this table feel the same way."

There were murmurs of assent from my colleagues. I heard Ricky Lee Washington say, "You got THAT right!"

Svoboda glared at me before speaking.

"I prefer to save the questions until the end. My presentation is timed precisely to fit in the time I was allotted for it. It will answer most of your questions, I am sure." Snap.

The next panel consisted of a Rube Goldberg-like maze of boxes and lines that appeared to be a revamped and enlarged research office. He had even given it a new name: The Directorate of Research and Technology. At first glance, Svoboda himself seemed to be heading it.

"Excuse me, Dr. Svoboda."

The good doctor now directed his glare at Chad Nunn.

"Am I to understand by the graphic that you would head the newly expanded research office? . . ."

"Directorate!" said Svoboda forcefully.

"Office," continued Nunn, "as well as being president of this university?"

"Precisely."

"And how in the hell would you do that?"

"I would have deputy directors, of course, but only I have the kind of connections—I prefer to think of it as clout—to bring in the large dollars we need to hire more researchers and construct the new research center.

"We have perfectly good research facilities in all of our research-oriented departments," said Chekhov, a physicist as well as our chairman. "They may be spread over a number of buildings, but they do exist."

"I will get to that in due course, sir." Snap.

Sure enough, the next graphic showed a plan for a new research tower and the demolishing of two existing buildings.

"Does that advocate what I think it advocates?" asked Alex Crandell. The State Board of Higher Education, which he represented on our committee, jealously guarded its power to pass judgment on what buildings were built and, presumably, torn down.

"Well, of course it does, or I would not have put it in my presentation," snapped Svoboda.

"Then I say, sir, that this would never fly! It would never fly!"

"You will see the wisdom of my plans when you see the rest of my presentation." Snap.

Svoboda continued to show us a maze of charts, graphs, and lists for another twenty minutes. Given his hostility to our earlier interruptions, the members quit saying anything. They adopted a "wake me when it's over" mentality. In Gloria Gordon's case, that was literally true. She snored softly through half of the presentation. The speaker either did not notice or chose not to pay attention to her somnolent state.

"Now, I would like to have a ten-minute break, and then I will take your written questions, to be sorted out by category by my assistant, Miss Petrie. He gestured to the hapless woman, who blinked and turned red in the face at the unaccustomed attention.

Dimitri Chekhov had had enough. Our normally mild-mannered chairman had reached his limit.

"The break is fine," he said. "But we will not write our questions out for you or Miss Petrie to sort through. Whether you realize it or not, a university president has to answer questions from a lot of publics. They can't be screened as to their difficulty. As President Truman said so wisely, 'The buck stops here' . . ." He pounded the table. "Or over in that corner office beyond that very wall." He gestured toward the president's office on the other side of the wall of the conference room.

Chekhov got up and motioned for Svoboda to follow him out of the room, presumably to the men's room down the hall. Miss Petrie followed her boss obediently, but presumably not into the men's room.

As the door opened, a waiter wheeled in a cart containing the coffee, tea, and pastries we were getting used to, and began setting out cups and plates. The committee members gathered in small groups, eating and drinking these refreshments.

I pulled Hadley aside. "This guy is a little out of touch with the real world," I whispered. "Too much time in government and the higher realms of corporate America."

"I guess the air gets so rarefied in some jobs that the people below you protect you from all unpleasantness," she responded.

"He sure doesn't know what we do here," I added. "He doesn't have a clue about most of it."

She nodded her head in agreement. "That's real apparent. He does not have a chance of being selected, as far as I can see. I'd never forward his name as a finalist."

"Nor would I," said Nunn, as he joined us. "He seems to have a real czar complex. He likes to think of himself at the top of all those boxes and lines. I have to be honest with you—he's a real asshole! Sorry, Hadley."

"A first-class asshole!" she laughed.

"One of the biggest assholes in the world," I added. "And I've known a lot of assholes!"

We all laughed heartily as Chekhov and Svoboda came back into the room, Miss Petrie close behind.

"Dr. Svoboda has agreed to take your questions verbally," Checkhov said. He sat down and the candidate stood up. At another finger snap, Miss Petrie placed a small lectern on the table in front of him, no doubt for a bit of protection from his audience. I always did the same for the first few weeks of class. Slings, arrows, and unpleasant questions bounced off more easily that way.

Victoria Chen was the first to speak.

"I repeat what Professor Martindale asked you earlier," she said. "What about undergraduate education? I came here because of its excellence, and I'm sure many of my fellow students feel the same way. I'm a long way from thinking about grad school."

"My dear Miss Chen," said Svoboda in a condescending way. "I am happy to see someone of your ethnic background on this committee. You should be proud of your heritage. Did your family migrate to one of the many Chinatowns? Worked on the railroad, did they?"

"Or maybe ran a laundry," she answered mockingly. "Actually my dad teaches at Stanford, and my mother is an attorney."

"Oh, excuse me for making a wrong assumption. I am . . ."

"A pretty racist dude," said Washington. This time, neither Chekhov nor anyone else jumped in to chastise him. "You got any room for a poor minority student like me in your city on a hill? Last time I looked, we got no hills on this campus. Lots of valleys, though."

Svoboda shifted uncomfortably, but did not respond.

"Is there a role for gender-specific women and men in your university?" asked Liz Stein.

"Gender specific?" said Svoboda.

"Lesbians and gay men."

"Oh, yes, I see. I have never heard that term before. Well, I had not given it much thought."

"I hate to say it, Dr. Svoboda," I interjected, "but there are many aspects of life at a university that you do not seem familiar with. I'm afraid it is very different from the government agencies and private companies you've been associated with."

"I am a quick learner, a quick study."

"I have no doubt about that," I said.

Svoboda's self-confidence seemed to be falling away rapidly. This was surprising, given his previous domination of the room. It almost seemed like he had caved in quickly under the slightest amount of pressure and challenge.

No more finger snaps. No more Miss Petrie with a new chart to save him.

After a few more rudimentary questions on mundane subjects, the committee ran out of things to ask Svoboda about. Chekhov put the candidate—and the rest of us—out of our collective misery.

"We thank you for your time and thoughtful presentation, Doctor Svoboda. We wish you and Miss Petrie a safe journey home. We stand adjourned."

* * *

There were three other candidates who did not make the final cut, and so were not invited to visit campus. I interviewed them over the telephone:

Margo Baines: *"I see Miss Baines, that you graduated from Vassar and then spent a year of graduate work at the Sorbonne in Paris, where you were a teaching assistant professor to Professor Phillippe André. Would it surprise you to know that Dr. André died the year before you were born?"*
"Well, er, ah, I . . . there has been a terrible mistake."
"Did you attend the Sorbonne, Miss Baines?"
Complete silence followed.

Alexander Shay: *"There is a lapse of two years in your vita, Dr. Shay. Can you fill in the time lapse from 1980 to 1982? It may be none of my business, but it does represent a substantial interruption to your career."*
Shay thought for a long time before he answered.
"You'll find out anyway, I guess. I was in the Missouri Hospital for the Criminally Insane during that time. But I'm much better now."

Harrison Andrews Johnson. *"I wonder if you could explain how you would manage the athletic department. You know it has a substantial deficit and a losing football team. How do you propose to deal with both of these problems? I mean, a winning team can really bring in new students and increase financial support from alumni and friends."*

"Football team. Athletics. I was not aware that there were problems. I specialized in Medieval Literature all of my career. But I'm a fast learner. I'll figure it out. I have no doubt about that."

21

Hancock and Maxine arrived separately to class the following Monday. If they had spent the previous night "doing it," as my students would say, they didn't act like it. They even sat in different seats lest anyone guess their growing infatuation.

"Good morning," I said. "I hope you all had a good weekend. I want to remind you that we will finish reading your articles this week, then go over the revisions next week. Remember, a key requirement in the course is that you write a query letter to a real magazine and mail it on the last day of this course. But you need to have the article ready to go if—or I should say, when—you get an acceptance. When we left here on Friday, Gary, you were reading your piece on the Vietnam War and your service. Do you feel like continuing or is it too painful?"

"No, professor. I'm good to go. I'm sorry I started slobbering. I guess real men do cry after all."

I dismissed the incident with a wave of my hand. "Not a problem. We were all moved by what you wrote."

"That's good. I'll get on with it then." He shuffled the pages and cleared his throat.

The use of herbicides continued for the rest of the war, although at reduced rates. The military tried to camouflage the true nature of the program—ultimately called Operation Ranch Hand because of the agricultural origins of the chemical compounds. It came to be known not as an eradication program but as a "food denial" program. The problem was the civilian population was being affected much more than the Vietcong, and they were getting sick besides and maybe having deformed babies.

From my seat high up in the airplane, I didn't know anything about this. I was following orders from above, using the justification that lower-level people always do to salve their consciences. I thought only of putting in my year in hell and going home. That was what was on my mind, not a bunch of gooks whose language I couldn't understand and whose lives were of little importance to me.

Later, though, I made a run with a buddy out of town to deliver the mail to Bien Ha Air Base, and we drove right through Tan Hiep. The village seemed deserted as we cruised into the city limits. Dogs lazed in the streets, barely willing to move when our vehicle reached them. Children peeked out at us from open doorways. Women turned their backs on us to continue to wash clothes.

After we had driven a few hundred yards, I noticed a figure dart out from behind a low wall and run toward our truck. She began shouting loudly at us in Vietnamese in that singsong manner I found impossible to learn. My friend slowed down so he would not hit her, and she kept coming at us. She was carrying some kind of package high in her arms.

> *"Holy shit," he shouted. "What the fuck does she want?"*
> *I turned in my seat to face her directly.*
> *"That's not a package, it's a baby," I shouted.*
> *At that point she threw the tiny bundle at me, and I caught it easily. I opened the blanket and recoiled at what I saw. The baby's face, contorted in anger and crying, was misshapen. Its left eye drooped, and its mouth seem to have been pulled to one side. The skin was black and dead looking with small pustules covering most of the skin.*

Hancock stopped reading and looked around at the rest of us. "That's as far as I got," he said. "I don't know how to end it."

"You poor man," said Edna Ruth Myers. "You've been through so much." She was not sitting near enough to him to reach over and pat his arm—her typical gesture of comfort— but I had no doubt that she would if given the chance.

"Powerful stuff," said Washington. "Bad times for y'all."

"Goll, like I don't know what to say," said Penelope Soriano, tears streaming down her cheeks.

"Ms. March, what is your reaction?"

She looked directly at me before she answered.

"I told Gary last night that this was the most powerful writing I'd ever read about the Vietnam War."

Why did she have to add that part about "last night"? It only confirmed something I had suspected. The two were sleeping together. I was angry at myself for the flash of jealousy that overcame me, but then I let it get the better of me.

"That seems a bit of an exaggeration," I said, avoiding her eyes and looking at Hancock. "The story you are telling is what is powerful. You lived through something horrible. Now you've got to bring the horror to your readers. I'm not sure you've done that yet. We need more passion and more facts. If you're going to make the story personal, you've got to take it really deep."

Was I being sincere or just letting my anger at her affect my judgment? I pressed ahead nonetheless.

"Another point to consider here is the market for yet another memoir of the Vietnam War. It means a lot to you because you lived through it. But will it mean anything to most readers? You need to study your markets."

"I can't believe how cruel you are, Professor Martindale," said Maxine. "This man has bared his soul to us, and all you can do is talk about markets!"

At that, she gathered her things and stood up. Flashing me a look of utter contempt, she walked out of the room and slammed the door.

22

For the past year or so, I had started hiking in the McDonald Forest any weekend I was free. Although this large experimental area is used by the College of Forestry primarily for research and teaching, it is also open to the public for recreation.

Because I had such a stressful week juggling presidential candidates and my teaching duties, I decided to put aside everything else I planned to do and spend this Saturday afternoon outdoors.

Against my better judgment, I invited Maxine March to go with me. Since she blew up at me in class, I hadn't seen her. But I found myself thinking about her at odd times of the day—and night. I decided that a face-to-face meeting might help me come to terms with the feelings I had for her. I called and invited her to go with me to the forest, and she accepted.

I had avoided personal entanglements for most of my life by putting them aside while I concentrated on my career. I couldn't seem to do that with her. Even though she was involved—apparently in a romantic way—with Hancock, I couldn't brush off my attraction to her.

I picked her up at her small house in the slightly rundown part of town south of Mary's River.

"Hi," she said sweetly, as she opened the door and got in my car. "I'm glad you called. I was facing a day of housework and assignments, so you rescued me from all of that. I also wanted to apologize for my behavior in class the other day."

"Don't think about it," I replied. "Just forget it happened. I have."

"I'm sort of impetuous sometimes," she said, as she smoothed her hair. She was dressed less provocatively than in class or at the beach, but there was no mistaking the beauty of her body under the blue work shirt and jeans.

I put the car in gear and drove back out to Highway 99W and turned north.

"I made us some lunch," she said.

"You did? That was very thoughtful. I planned to stop off for some fast food."

"Fast food for a fast guy?"

"You could say that, but you'd be wrong."

I always blushed easily and did so now. Why did this woman bring out the schoolboy in me? She ignored my obvious discomfort and looked straight ahead.

"Great day. I can't wait to spend some time outdoors. I'm a big city girl, but I love the outdoors. My family always spent summers on a lake in northern Michigan. I lived for those weeks outside."

"Yeah, I love being outdoors, too. So, how's school going?"

"I love your class, and I'm also taking beginning French. I need to brush up on my conversational skills."

"Are you going to France?"

"Yes, in the fall. Duncan said he would pay for a trip."

I felt a twinge of jealousy at the mention of Delgado's name. That was ridiculous. I barely knew this woman, and the two of them had been married. I had no right to feel jealous or anything else about Maxine.

"You and he will be going together?"

"Are you kidding! He wouldn't be caught dead with me in public. By the terms of our divorce settlement, he has to pay me so much a year. Mostly that comes in the form of a monthly check, but sometimes he throws in some extras, like a plane ticket. He probably has Frequent Flyer miles or something he needed to get rid of. He wouldn't buy me a ticket to Paris, France—or even Paris, Texas—just to be nice! That's for sure!"

All this insider stuff about her marriage was interesting, but it was making me nervous.

"I think you'll like the forest. It should be cooler out there today than here in town. We can hike up to an area I know that's near a waterfall. It'll be a good place to eat."

"Sounds wonderful."

She had untied her scarf so that her hair would fall down— it reached to just below her shoulders. We rode in silence for several miles, enjoying the day. I opened the sunroof of my car to allow the sun and the gentle breeze to reach us.

I turned onto the side road that led to the forest. Soon, we were driving through the gate and past the rustic building used for conferences and meetings. I parked in the lot beyond the small pond; only service vehicles were allowed on the roads in the forest itself.

"I've got a blanket and some folding chairs in the trunk," I said, as I got out. "Some iced tea, too."

"Sounds good to me," she said, as she opened the door and grabbed the basket of food she had stashed in the back seat.

I led the way out of the parking lot and onto the path around the pond.

"This is absolutely beautiful," she said.

"You look more relaxed already."

"I do feel the tiredness draining away. I've been so tense for months."

We walked up to the chain across the roadway. I took the basket from her and helped her step across.

"How gallant," she smiled.

"I thought so."

I kept hold of the basket and her hand.

"Why, Professor Martindale," she laughed. "Are you holding my hand?"

What was happening to me? I was feeling ridiculous. Grown men don't behave like teenage boys! I dropped her hand.

"Remember, I was being gallant."

"Oh, of course. I forgot."

We walked up the roadway, pausing every now and then to look at a plant, a squirrel, and a doe in the distance.

"They're so cautious," she said.

"Can you imagine being on guard like that all the time?" I said.

"Tell me about it," she said with a knowing look. "I'm a real expert."

" Are you that scared of Duncan?"

She sniffed the air and took a deep breath. "Let's not spoil the day by talking about unpleasant subjects. Believe me, he's a real unpleasant subject!"

We walked on in silence for a few more yards.

"This is where I've been heading," I said to break the silence. "Right over here by that fallen tree."

"Wow. Did they cut it down?"

"Oh, no, not here. They'd never do that in such a careless way. Lightning probably caused it."

We reached the log and I put everything down.

"Makes a good picnic table, don't you think?"

I straddled the log and motioned for Maxine to do the same.

Fire had burned out a section along the top of the log. Imperfect as it was, it made a good resting place for our food. Maxine proceeded to unpack the basket.

"I fried some chicken and made some potato salad." She brought out two plastic containers and pried off the lids, then she handed me a plate, and napkin, and a spoon.

"There are some cookies in there for later."

"I had no idea you were so domestic," I laughed, taking a bite of the chicken breast. "I love this. Really good. White meat's the best!"

"How do you feel about breasts?" she laughed.

"I'm all for them, too," I replied.

We both ate in silence for a while, enjoying the outdoor setting and each other's company.

"I want you to know that I don't usually socialize with my students," I said. "It's not a good thing to do."

"So you've said countless times. Are you afraid of them?" She was holding back a smile, but I could see amusement in her eyes.

"Are you mocking me, Ms. March? Most of my students are a lot younger than you. In the academic world, we call that moral turpitude."

"Are you saying I'm old?" She was frowning now.

"Old enough not to report any transgression I might commit against you or with you or whatever." Two could play this sparring game.

"What kind of transgression did you have in mind?"

"Give me a little time, and I'm sure I'll think of something," I laughed.

"I can hardly wait."

She leaned over and kissed me on the cheek. And I put my arms around her and kissed her on the mouth, a real smooch.

"Whew," she sighed. "That was nice."

"I say again that not only do I not go on picnics with my students, I don't kiss them, while I am on those picnics that I don't go on either."

"Now even I know that's a convoluted sentence," she laughed. "You feel like a little roll in the hay, so to speak?" she said. "I know, I know, you don't want to get your clothes dirty. I'll tell you what. I'll wash them for you."

We were still facing each other on the log, but had long since removed the food. I placed both hands on her shoulders and drew her toward me. Then I kissed her again more passionately and for a longer time.

"Let me come up for air," she said breathlessly, fanning herself in a mocking way. "You're a pretty good kisser."

"Thanks, but I'm kind of out of practice. In my monk-like existence, I don't often get the chance."

"But not for lack of offers, I'd bet. You ever been married, Tom?

"No. Never."

"What a loss to the ladies who are running around frustrated and single."

"I'd hardly put myself in that kind of category. I'm getting too old and set in my ways to make a good catch for anyone."

"I don't agree," she replied. "You're rich, handsome, and smart. What more can a girl ask for?"

I got off the log. "Naw. I'm a bad risk. I work all the time. I snore. And I'm sure you've had many lovers better than I'd ever be able to become."

"That's for me to find out, and then I'll be the judge."

I shook my head.

"I can't do it. I like you—a lot. But it would be much too messy for me."

"You always need for things to be neat and tidy? Life's not that way. It's never tied up in neat little packages with velvet ribbon. Believe me, if my life is any example, everything is usually tied up with rubber bands or cheap string."

"I think you've had more than your share of bad luck, but I'm not in a position to do much about that."

"That's not the position I had in mind."

"Is that a leer?" I laughed.

"You bet! If it gets you to throw away your inhibitions—and your clothes, of course—and go with the moment. Come over here, and I'll help you unbutton your shirt and undo your zipper."

"Sorry. Time to pack up and get back to town."

I folded the blanket and started putting the remains of the food and the plates and napkins and forks into the basket.

"You're no fun at all," she said, pretending to pout.

"It's better that we be friends, not lovers. Things are never quite the same after a man and woman spend the night together."

"That's what I'm counting on."

Beyond my worry over the impropriety of making out with a student—even a student nearly as old as I am—was the worry over how Duncan Delgado would react if he found out that I was screwing his ex-wife. From all I had seen, he had a volatile temper. When he heard the news—probably from her, as a way to wound his Latin machismo—he would not behave well.

As I rounded up the rest of the stuff to carry back to the car, a loud explosion quite literally knocked me off my feet and onto the ground. Maxine fell off the other side of the log she was still sitting on. Birds on the nearby trees took to the air, chattering their dismay at being disturbed. I rushed to Maxine's side.

"Are you okay?"

I helped her up, and she started brushing herself off.

"That was an explosion of some kind. It wasn't just some logging class blasting stumps," I said excitedly.

As I headed into the forest behind where we had been sitting, I smelled smoke. I ran as fast as I could up the hill, dodging the brush that had overgrown the path. By the time I got to the top of the hill, I could see white puffs of smoke coming from an area of the forest that was so dense, I could not see through it from where I had stopped. I continued on and then the path ran out.

As I pressed ahead, I had to slow down because I needed to part the tree limbs and other brush that was in my way. I reached a clearing after a few more minutes and paused to get my bearings. The smoke was coming from the engine of a car that was sitting in the middle of the clearing. Something had exploded in that engine and then singed, but not completely burned up, the rest of the vehicle. The car was blackened, but still intact. Even though the forest was tinder dry at this time of year, the flames had put themselves out and not ignited any of the trees.

I approached the car from the back, hoping to find it empty. Logic would dictate otherwise, however. No one would torch a car unless . . . I didn't want to think about it, but knew I would have to do just that in a few seconds.

My heart was racing as I walked along the driver's side of the car. It was a two-door Ford Escort of uncertain age. I had owned one myself in my leaner years.

I stopped at the door and looked through the shattered glass. The figure inside did not seem to be moving, but I had to be certain. I took off my shirt and wadded it up to act as protection for my hand. I pulled hard on the door, and it gave way quickly.

Because the body inside had been leaning against the door, the movement of opening it caused the body to topple sideways. As it hit the ground, the charred flesh on the neck and throat all but disintegrated, as did the bone and cartilage beneath.

As neatly as if it had been under the blade of a guillotine, the head dislodged itself from the body and rolled toward the edge of the clearing.

Driver's license says he's Hector Morales. Lived in Albany."

Angela Pride looked as immaculate as she always did. Even though she was walking through the charred remains of the car and the scorched area around it, she did not have so much as a smudge on her Oregon State Police coveralls. She held the wallet up in one of her gloved hands before dropping it into an evidence bag.

I had called Angela because I knew her well, but I also figured she would have primary jurisdiction over this forest, which was university property.

"Who's that woman, Tom? She looks familiar."

"Her name is Maxine March. You met her at the Coast last year."

"Oh, yeah, I remember. She had the hots for you as I recall, but you weren't interested." Angela smiled at the memory. "I think you said I saved you from her clutches."

Angela chuckled. Seeing her under these circumstances was more than a little awkward. It made me feel odd to have her see me out here in the woods with Maxine. I ignored the taunt.

"We came out here to hike and have a picnic."

"Not like you to do anything too strenuous, Tom." Angela was smiling, but she knew me all too well. "She's one of your students. Part-time, I assume?"

I nodded.

Angela's probing questions had very little to do with her investigation, but I answered them without hesitation. I learned a long time ago that it was better to be up front with her or she would trip you up later.

"Does she have a job?"

"Actually, I don't think she has a job. She's divorced. Maybe she lives on alimony."

"She's a little long in the tooth to be a student, isn't she, Tom?"

Women have their ways of dissing other women. Angela's stiletto was definitely out.

"She's just taking one or two courses, I think."

"Something to do while she waits for her next alimony check, no doubt."

Why was Angela carrying on so much about Maxine? It couldn't be jealousy. We hadn't been an item for a couple of years.

"She had no involvement with the decedent?" Angela got back to the matter at hand.

"I doubt it, but you'll have to ask her. I know something about him. I'd even seen him."

She looked surprised. "And how did that happen?"

"I was on jury duty last year, and his was the case we were considering. I think he killed someone when he tried to rob a jewelry store."

"So did you find him guilty or what?"

"I wasn't picked as a juror, so I don't know."

I decided not to tell Angela about my visit with Morales's attorney. That had no bearing on this, or even if it did, I'd keep it to myself for now. Angela would go ballistic if she found out, but maybe she wouldn't find out.

"So it's a coincidence that you and your . . . um . . . friend were here when a car exploded and a man died?"

"That's what I'm saying. How would I have anything to do with an exploding car?"

"I remember that your own car exploded once, after it rolled off a cliff in the forest near Newport," she said. "Strange things do happen when you are around, Tom. You have to admit it."

"I was being chased by a man who was trying to kill me," I said, a bit heatedly. "How was that my fault?"

"I guess you're right, but it might bear looking into." There was a rare twinkle in Angela's eyes. She was normally very serious about her work with no time for humor of any kind, but she did like to rattle my chain from time to time.

"Yeah, I'd bring in the FBI and Interpol, if I were you!"

Her face broke into a big smile.

"Let me talk to Ms. . . ."—she looked at her notebook—". . . March. It won't take long. Then you can take her home—or to your home—or wherever. Get her away from this gruesome scene."

"Great. Thanks, Angela."

She walked away from me toward Maxine, who was sipping something from a steamy paper cup. She stopped and turned, "And Tom?"

"Yes?"

"Don't leave town." Another big grin.

"Only if I take you along to keep tabs on me."

"That's the best offer I've had in, let's see, two years."

Maxine stood up when Angela got to her. I wasn't close enough to hear what was being said, but I watched them out of the corner of my eye while I concentrated on the men working the area around the car. They had carefully hung tape that said "POLICE LINES—DO NOT CROSS" around the area that was blackened by the blast and subsequent fire.

A few technicians were on their hands and knees sifting through the pine needles on the ground; two more were working around the body itself and the interior of the car. A third man was taking photos of everything from various angles.

Angela was writing down what Maxine told her. Maxine gestured toward the area where we had sat on the log to eat. Then she swung her arm in an arc, I suppose to indicate how we had seen and heard the blast before running over.

After five minutes or so, Angela closed her notebook and handed Maxine her business card. Then they both walked over to me.

"You are both free to go, Tom. Ms. March has been extremely helpful. She's not into obstructing justice like you always are."

"Or perjury," I added. "I love perjury. I try to think of ways to perjure myself and lie to the police. Constantly."

"On that somber note, I will bid you both a good afternoon," said Angela unsmilingly.

She joined the others in the area by the car. I took Maxine by the arm and led her down the path to where we had sat on the log. Once there, we picked up the remains of our picnic lunch and carried them to my car.

"She's still in love with you," said Maxine, as we walked along.

"What did you say?"

"The policewoman. Anna? Alice?"

"Angela."

"Angela, yeah. Didn't you say the two of you were an item?"

"Yes, on and off up until two years ago."

"Well, I'm saying she still likes you—a lot. She'd like to get back together with you."

I shrugged and shook my head. "I doubt that."

"I could tell by the way she reacted when she was close to you. She'd like to get very close to you again. Like in bed."

"I feel very uncomfortable talking to you about this. I'm your professor."

"Don't pull rank on me."

"I've finished talking about it." The conversation was making me very uncomfortable. Getting back to the incident, I asked, "Did you have anything to contribute to her investigation?"

"Maybe a little."

I stopped walking. "You did? Now *that* is real news!"

"I've heard Morales's name before. From Duncan. I was in his office a few weeks ago when he answered the phone while his secretary was on a break. He was speaking in Spanish, which I understand, although he doesn't know it. He got very angry at whoever it was, but I know he called him Hector."

"How will Duncan react when he finds out that you mentioned this to the police?"

"Look, Tom. I am sick to death of living my life in fear of Duncan Delgado. This will be my first step out from under his shadow. I need to establish a life of my own and not live in fear of him."

She sounded very brave and resolute, but what she had done made me shudder. Several times during the drive back to town, I reached over and patted her hand.

In reality, though, my mind was on commencement the next day. And once that was behind me, I was looking forward to bringing this interminable presidential search to an end.

PART THREE

The Search for Murder—
and a Murderer—Is Over
June 12 to June 21, 2005

For a few seconds, I was too stunned to move. Amid the screams and shouting from others behind me in the box, I reached over to check Joseph Svoboda's pulse, even though I was sure he had died instantly. I sat where I was for the time being, fearful that another shot might hit me.

"I'm a doctor, let me through," said a voice behind me.

I stood up numbly and moved aside to let a short, squat man wearing a university cap in closer.

"Tony North. You okay?"

"Yeah, yeah, fine. How'd you get here so fast?"

"My kid's graduating, and I heard the shot and saw the other guy fall. He's dead for sure."

In all the pandemonium, I had forgotten about Ray Blandings. I peered over the edge of the box in time to see paramedics covering his body. He was lifted onto a stretcher and carried out of sight to the rear of the stadium and away in an ambulance.

I looked out at the once orderly stadium floor. Somehow, the faculty marshals had been able to keep the students from fleeing in all directions. They were marching out in pretty much the reverse order of how they had come in. The platform party was gone, although no one in it had ever been in danger because the shots had come from the unfinished side of the stadium behind them.

Suddenly the band started playing "The Stars and Stripes Forever." The music had a calming effect on the scene below. It seemed as though the stirring melody had brought everyone to the realization that the danger was over.

"I assume you didn't get hit, since I don't see blood pouring from any of your orifices." Paul Bickford stood next to me in a spot I would swear was empty seconds before.

"Major Stealth, I presume. Yeah, my orifices are not oozing, at this moment at least. What do you know?"

Bickford glanced around before answering. "Two dead, a couple of minor injuries to people in the crowd when they panicked and tried to climb over seats. For the most part, though, I'm amazed. People went about their business in a pretty orderly way. This could have been a disaster, but it wasn't."

"Your guy, Chang, is all right?"

"In a helicopter to Portland as we speak. He was not the intended target. My guess is it's a homegrown guy with a grudge against these two candidates."

"Svoboda I can see, but Blandings? He was a meek guy who didn't seem the type to make enemies," I said.

"Maybe not here, but maybe before. I need to screen those files I sent you and dig deeper."

"You're going to be involved with the investigation? This isn't a federal matter. Why you?"

"Your friend Lieutenant Pride asked me to assist her, along with the locals and the Oregon State Police," he said.

"That'll be good to have your expertise. I'd like to be a part of . . ."

"Tom, you are not a trained law-enforcement professional, although you act like one much of the time," said Bickford.

"You're kidding. You think I've butt in too much—I look at it as . . ."

". . . fun to play cops and robbers. I look at it as interference that becomes a royal pain in the ass."

"Sometimes it has helped in the past," I protested. "Angela credits me with . . ."

"She said you put yourself in danger, and she always has to get you out of whatever mess you've gotten into," he said.

"You talked to her about me?"

He nodded. "Last night over dinner."

"You bastard. You're horning in on my territory."

"She said you broke up several years ago."

"That's right, but that doesn't mean that I . . ."

"That doesn't mean you have any reason to protest or care about anything she does," he continued.

"Are you stealthful in bed, too, major?"

"I do believe you're jealous, professor."

He glanced around the box which was nearly empty. Security people had hustled Mrs. Sykes, Lillian White, and the other guests out quickly and onto the elevator.

"I'm wasting time here. Glad you're safe. I will call you tomorrow and let you know what I find out about those guys. There's bound to be something I missed."

Bickford walked quickly up the steps and out the door before I could say anything else. I felt drained of all energy and heartsick at what had happened. A maniac with a gun had ruined one of the nicest events of the year. I looked down and picked up my program. Spatters of blood marred the cover. I threw it down as quickly as I had picked it up. I would not need any such memento to remember this horrible day.

✳   ✳   ✳

At Angela Pride's suggestion, we met the following morning in her office in the security building next to the railroad tracks.

"Coffee anyone?"

I raised my hand and Bickford nodded. Angela walked around the table to fill our cups.

"Black for you, Tom. Major?"

"The same."

Angela sat down behind her desk and took a sip of coffee before speaking.

"Against my better judgment, Tom, I wanted to brief you on what we know about yesterday's unfortunate incident. Given your past history of meddling . . ." She smiled at me and I shrugged my shoulders. ". . . I was leery. But Major Bickford convinced me to bring you into the loop. You are running the search committee and are familiar with the backgrounds of the people who were killed. Maybe you can help us figure out why these men were targeted."

"I am grateful," I said. "And I do feel responsible—not that they were killed, but that we brought them into a place of danger."

Bickford moved his arm in a gesture of dismissal. "No one could have predicted that this would become a 'place of danger,' as you call it. Our killer made it that, and we had no way of knowing in advance."

"But you need to promise me . . . "—Angela glanced at Bickford—". . . us, that you won't do any of your typical big-footing. No amateur detective work that puts your life in danger and, at the same time, jeopardizes the investigation."

"I'm not admitting that I did anything of that nature in the past," I laughed, "but I agree not to do whatever it is you think I might have done."

"I thought journalists were supposed to write and speak clearly," said Bickford, a deadpan look on his face.

"Convoluted sentences are good at times," I replied. "Keeps your audience on its toes."

"Let's get on to this incident," said Angela. "We can exchange clever remarks later."

Both Bickford and I sat up straight and folded our hands in front of us. This was serious stuff, and I did not really feel all that jocular.

"Any trace of the killer?" I asked them.

"He got away before we could get to the other side," said Angela. "We think he was on one of those huge gantry cranes, but aren't sure at this point."

"But you had guys all over the place," I continued.

"Fewer on that side because it was behind the stage," said Bickford. "Don't forget, I was charged with protecting General Chang. No one else was at risk, as far as I knew."

"We're combing the area under the cranes and will send someone up on both of them later today," said Angela.

"Both Svoboda and Blandings were candidates for the presidency of this university," I said. "Svoboda came from the outside, but had no record at this university that could come back to haunt him."

"That we know of," said Bickford.

"Yes, Tom, that we know of," Angela said, agreeing with Bickford. "Blandings, on the other hand, had been on the faculty here for years. Did he make any local enemies?"

"I doubt it, but I don't know that for certain," I said. "Ray was a nice guy who didn't seem the type to have enemies. You make a lot of hard decisions as a dean, but you seldom make decisions that will drive someone to murder you. I mean, you don't haul out a high-powered rifle because you're angry over not getting tenure or being promoted. We can be vicious here, but we wound with words, not bullets. It just doesn't fit."

"I agree with Tom, Lieutenant Pride," said Bickford. "It's something beyond the campus. I'll go deeper into Dean Blandings's background."

"What do we know about Svoboda?" she asked.

"He was a control freak and very authoritarian in the way he treated the committee. I think he was very smart, but he wore that intelligence on his sleeve and liked to show it off every chance he had. One of those guys who had his IQ tattooed on his forehead. I don't think anyone on the committee liked him all that much. He seemed out of the running for a while, until we ran out of finalists."

"But what about his background?" asked Bickford. "What did he do before he applied for this job?"

"To tell you the truth, we got so hung up on his wish list, we barely talked about his background. It was in engineering and business, I think. He was one of those guys who is brought in when a company is dying or in bankruptcy to stop the bleeding. I guess he's used to getting his way and spending whatever it takes to accomplish the overall salvage operation. He banks on people being so grateful, they don't question anything he does."

"Which companies?" asked Angela.

"I'd have to look at the file. I don't remember. I, for one, decided on the spot that he was not our guy."

"Why invite him to commencement ?" asked Bickford.

"Despite our reservations, we invited him back for another interview along with Lillian White. Blandings was there as a courtesy and had been told he was not being considered for the job. This kind of thing happens a lot with searches. You wind up with people who are not perfect. That's what happened with Svoboda."

"Our shooter had to be tracking their schedules to know where they'd be," Bickford continued.

"The schedules were all public," I said. "Everything we do here is done in the open. It would be easy for anyone to figure out how to find either guy. So, where do we begin?"

"*We* don't begin anything," said Angela, emphatically. "Remember your promise."

"Oh, yeah, I got carried away."

Bickford looked at his watch. "I've got to get to Portland to be in on a briefing session via closed-circuit TV regarding this incident. I'll run Svoboda and Blandings through a number of checks and see what we get. I'll be back here tomorrow—can we meet again then, say, same time, same place? Let's lose the professor, lieutenant." Bickford's face was impassive. I started to speak but he held up his hand to stop me. "Maybe we can stretch the rules a bit one more day."

Angela smiled her assent.

"Why do you guys torment me at every turn?" I asked.

"Who knows," Bickford said on his way out the door, "maybe you were the intended target."

We all laughed at that frivolous remark, but in the back of my mind, I wondered if Delgado had targeted me because of my involvement with Maxine and because I had upset his experiments with the illegals.

* * *

Later that day, I returned to my office to read the final articles from the magazine writing class. With grades due on Friday, I needed to finish by tomorrow at the latest. As was my custom, I read the articles in no particular order.

Edna Ruth Meyers wrote her predictable piece on her family history in eastern Oregon. The writing was not bad, but the subject was just not very interesting to anyone other than her family. I was careful to be constructive in my comments on her writing. She had a very grammatically correct but dull style that no magazine editor would touch. I noted a few Western history publications that might be worth a query. I gave the article a "B."

Ricky Lee Washington had a writing style as unruly as his behavior in the classroom and the search committee meetings. Behind the anger and the arrogance, however, there were some patches of good writing.

> *Children who grow up in a ghetto have more strikes against them than the last batter up on the final game of the World Series.*
>
> *"It is a miracle that any child of color who lives in such dire circumstances ever achieves anything but a life filled with violence and poverty," said Dr. Henriette St. Germain, professor of psychology at Oregon University.*
>
> *According to the 2000 Census, one out of four Black children in the United States lives in a household where the income is below the national poverty line.*
>
> *La Marva Brooks should know. The eight-year-old girl from Portland never knew her father. Her mother works two jobs to put food on the table for La Marva and brother Baylee, aged five.*

I was pleased and proud of Ricky's article. He had done everything I had taught him to do. His writing was smooth and the facts were presented in an interesting way. I made only a few suggested changes and gave him an "A."

Penelope Soriano's piece was pretty bad. It was as if she had not listened to anything I said all term or read the textbook. I tried not to dump on her too much as I slashed away whole paragraphs and circled misspelled words. I did not think the world was waiting with baited breath to read the history of her sorority, complete with her gushing comments on her own membership. If it hadn't been the final assignment, I would have let her revise it.

"Too late for that," I muttered, as I put a "C" in the upper right corner.

Instead of a completed assignment, I got a neatly typed note from Maxine March. I hadn't seen her since our disastrous picnic in McDonald Forest last week, what with commencement and the search.

> *Dear Professor Martindale—I am sorry that I can't turn in my final assignment in your magazine writing course. I have to leave town unexpectedly for a while. I do plan to finish the article and get it to you as soon as I can. Until that time, I want to ask that you give me the grade of incomplete.*
>
> *Thank you for understanding. I know you are a very understanding person and I hope you will forgive me.*
>
> *Sincerely yours,*
> *Maxine March*

The tone and content were certainly what I would want in case someone else read the note. There was no hint that anything personal had occurred between us. Actually, nothing had—except in my head and heart. But that was my business. I wondered why she had left so suddenly without calling me. I also wondered where she was headed.

Gary Hancock's finished piece was my last one to grade. He had made all the changes I suggested in class. The result was a compelling article that captured well the plight of Vietnam vets. It was informative and poignant. I felt it might evoke sympathy in readers for a group of men long neglected in the U.S.

He hadn't had an ending in his earlier draft. He had added one in this final revision.

> *All that is wrong with thousands of veterans of the Vietnam War can be traced to a small cabal of men who raped the land in that tiny country with their lethal herbicides. The residue of that poison then ruined the lives of hundreds of Americans forced to live and fight on the terrain sprayed from above. May the owners and managers of Lone Star Chemical rot forever in the same kind of hell!*

I reached for the phone to call both Paul Bickford and Angela Pride.

My first inclination was to wait for Paul and Angela to get back to me with the results of their database searches. But maybe they wouldn't get back to me. I recalled Angela's admonition to me not to "bigfoot" into this case.

I felt partially responsible for what had happened and felt strongly that I had to try to figure out who had killed two people and barely missed me. If I went back to where the shootings had occurred, maybe I would find something the investigators had missed.

* * *

Although students overuse the word "awesome" constantly, it did apply to the newly renovated football stadium on the southern edge of campus. At a cost of $80 million, it was the largest construction project in the history of the county. The expanded stands would add eight thousand more seats to handle happy alums who wanted to cheer on their team. Although no one ever donated that much money for academics, even a nonsports fanatic like me had to admit that the athletic program influenced all elements of the university. If the football team was winning, people were more inclined to donate money and send their children here. It reverberated in many directions.

I strolled nonchalantly along the street in front of the stadium, looking for all the world like someone enjoying a pleasant summer evening. In reality, I was looking for an unlocked gate or some opening in the fence that I could slip through. Even though the construction was not quite complete, security had been relaxed slightly. I saw no security guards. The shootings were being treated as an isolated incident, not really linked to the stadium. The investigation had moved elsewhere.

At the south end of the new grandstand, I found what I was looking for: a small gap between the edge of the structure and the temporary chain-link fence that extended up to it. I eyed the space and decided that I could safely make it through— hopefully without getting stuck. I sucked in my gut and tried. My only problem was that my belt buckle got stuck.

As I pulled myself back out, I heard a car coming down the street. I ducked behind a nearby shed and watched as a campus security car rolled by slowly. Had its occupant seen me?

I held my breath.

The car slowed down and stopped.

More breath holding.

A security man got out and seemed headed for me. In fact, he walked up to the shed and tried the door on the opposite side from where I was crouched. As I waited, I tried to think of a logical explanation for being here—as usual in the wrong place at the wrong time.

Just then, a staccato noise came from the radio in his car. He grunted and walked quickly to it. I took that opportunity to come out of hiding, remove my belt, and slip through the gap I had been unable to navigate before.

I checked on the security guard after I got inside, just in time to hear him start his car and drive off. With that concern gone, I walked along the rear of the stadium and soon found an elevator. Miraculously, it was not locked.

After the door opened, I pressed the button for the top level and waited while it sped me there. I might have been in a high-rise in a large city anywhere in the country. It was hard to fathom that I was on a campus that, twenty years ago when I first arrived, had only one or two elevators.

When I reached the top, the door opened with the usual bell and I stepped out, into a long hall. Suites were on my left, restrooms on my right. I had read that these private sanctums cost over $40,000 for a season and were sold out. The one on the opposite side of the stadium that had been occupied by the president's party at commencement had seemed posh to me, but these new ones probably outdid it in luxury and convenience.

At the end of the hallway, I saw a door that I hoped would lead me even higher and to the perch the killer had used. I opened it and found myself at the top of the fire exit; wide stairways headed down, and a more narrow one went up. At the top, I opened yet another door and stepped out onto the roof, ignoring the NO ADMITTANCE sign.

I was looking for any sign that Hancock had been up here and done the shooting. Even though I was sure the police had combed the area for anything left behind by the shooter, I had to satisfy my curiosity.

On the roof, I was standing at the base of one of the huge gantry cranes used to construct the grandstand—the one where the shooter had done his deadly work. These large structures, part of the university's skyline for over a year, would soon be moved to another job in another city.

I scanned the area under this crane for anything that might have dropped from above.

Nothing.

I saw no choice but to go even higher. To do this, I used the construction elevator—less imposing than the permanent one I had exited minutes before, but designed well enough to get the job done. I climbed in, closed the cage-like door, and pressed the button with an UP arrow on it. It lurched upward rather jerkily and then stopped at the top. I got out and stepped onto the roof. I had read in the material prepared for commencement that the roof was 150 feet above the playing field, the equivalent of the height of a twelve-story building.

Despite a mild case of acrophobia, I walked to the edge to look across to the other side, the dim outline of the hills beyond, and the twinkling lights of the city. I did not look straight down, however.

I scanned the rooftop with my penlight and found it clear of any construction debris. There was also nothing under the crane. I had assumed that the shooter had fired from this side of the structure, given our position across the field in the president's box.

As an afterthought, I walked across to the other end and repeated my search. This time, the light caught the reflection of something shiny. I walked over to it and picked it up. I turned it over my hand without recognizing it.

"An Air Force sharpshooting medal," said a voice behind me. "I think you'll agree that I am good at what I do—at least one thing I do."

Gary Hancock stepped out from behind one of the lattice-enclosed struts that held up the roof. He was carrying a rifle.

"I'm surprised you're still around," I said. "I mean, returning to the scene of the crime and all that."

He smiled ruefully. "The medal fell out of my pocket when I ran away the other day. I needed to get it back. I always carry it with me. How'd you guess it was me?"

"I didn't know for sure at first. But the more I thought about it, the more I realized that your anger and anguish over the war sets you apart. People today are angry and upset about more recent events, like the war in Iraq, but Vietnam has pretty much faded away from the national scene except for . . ."

"Nut cases like me," he laughed. " 'Nam changed my life. You might say it ruined my life. It was those fuckin' chemical companies that ruined everything." Tears filled his eyes.

"I just don't get the link between the men you killed and what happened to you."

"Fuckin' Blandings was a research chemist at Lone Star. He's responsible for so much hurt in the world, I can't even begin to tell you about it."

"How'd you find him?"

"A bunch of us vets have set up an informal network where we share information on the people who screwed us over in 'Nam. When we find one through Internet searches and other research, we try to render justice."

"You mean by killing them?"

He thought for a moment. "I think you know the answer to that."

"If you were aiming for Blandings, why'd you kill Svoboda?"

Hancock smiled. "Actually, professor, I was aiming at you."

Suddenly I felt weak in the knees, and my throat became very dry. Hancock pulled me over to the edge of the roof.

"I figured you found me out," he said. "And my work wasn't finished. I really need to complete this job. I owe it to my buddies and all those innocent people in Vietnam. Sorry. Nothing personal."

Hancock stepped back and raised his rifle.

"If you close your eyes, it'll be less scary," he said. "You won't anticipate when the bullet will hit you."

"I can't say that's a comforting thought." As usual, I had gone into my whistling past the graveyard mode.

"I promise you won't feel a thing."

I hadn't thought my life would end this way, but who can ever predict precisely the time of their own demise? There certainly wouldn't be much left to bury—as my grandmother used to say, nothing but a grease spot. I closed my eyes.

"This is really hard for me, professor. You're a decent man. You've been kind to me."

As I heard him cock the rifle, I spread my legs apart slightly, why I did not know. I would fall over the edge pretty fast, no matter how I was standing.

The rifle fired, and I waited for what I figured would be overwhelming pain. It didn't happen. I opened my eyes.

Hancock fell where he was, his rifle clattering and bouncing slightly on the roof.

"You owe me yet again for saving your sorry ass," said Paul Bickford, as he stepped out of the shadows, lowering a pistol.

"My ass was not what I was worried about," I said, stepping back from the edge.

I always seem to have a lot of unanswered questions whenever I'm involved in dicey situations—"situations" is the best I can come up with to describe what I had just been through. Since I'm not a trained law-enforcement person, "cases" is way exaggerated. Angela Pride, perhaps aptly, calls them "messes."

At any rate, the latest "whatever" was over. Even though I had been in the middle of most of the action, there was still a great deal I did not know.

"Why did Hancock shoot Blandings and Svoboda?" I asked.

Angela took a sip of coffee before answering. We were sitting in her office a week after commencement and my near-death encounter with Hancock on the roof of the stadium. "We're still piecing it together but it looks like he was aiming at both you and Blandings. Svoboda just got in the way."

"That's what he said on the roof, I mean about Blandings. I wasn't sure whether to believe him or not," I said.

"Hancock found out that Blandings once worked for Lone Star, a chemical company he had wrapped up all his antiwar hatred in. I guess that set him off, and he decided he could avenge all the wrongs of the Vietnam War if he killed someone he felt had somehow been responsible. In reality, Blandings was nothing more than a low-level chemist in those years, just starting his career. He might not even have been involved in herbicide research."

"Obsessive people don't always reason things out," I said. "Why me? He said he thought I had found him out. Was that it?"

"How well do you know Maxine March?"

"Do you always answer a question with another question?"

Angela didn't say anything.

"I told you a bit about her before. She asked for my help a number of months ago in finding a good class. She wound up taking one of mine. Hancock was in the same class, they met and, I presume, started dating. They had their antiVietnam War past in common."

"She was involved in demonstrations?"

"Yes, right in the thick of the 1968 Democratic convention in Chicago. She met her future husband, Duncan Delgado, there."

"But you saw her out of class."

I hesitated.

"Look, Tom, I saw the two of you having a picnic in McDonald Forest a few weeks ago. Last year, I saw her without her shirt in your house at the coast. I saw what I saw. The two of you were not engaging in reading and conference."

"Okay, I'll admit it. I find her attractive. She's hardly a conventional student. She's our age. I broke my own rule, I guess."

"I'd say you did just that," she smiled, with a rueful shake of her head. "I'd say you were in love with her."

"I wouldn't go that far. I'm too old to fall in love."

"Okay, Tom, maybe not love but some nice sex."

Angela was getting angry over this. Her usual professional demeanor was slipping away.

"I'm not really sure what I was after, if you want to know the truth, Angela. At first, I resisted her — like at the coast. Then I took her on the picnic. You were there when that ended. I did not have sex with her. It never went that far. I guess I liked her company. She seemed lonely and in need of someone to talk to."

"Did you know she was having an affair with Hancock?"

"I wasn't sure, but I assumed as much." I was getting nervous and wondering where this was going.

"And how did you reach that conclusion?"

"I saw them together in class and one other time."

"And that was when?"

"Am I being interrogated here?"

"I'm just trying to sort things out."

"About what? Has something happened to Maxine?"

"Just answer the question, Tom."

I did not like the direction this was taking.

"Tom?"

"I went to her apartment a few weeks ago and saw them go in together. He didn't leave right away."

"Meaning you staked out the place."

"I wanted to chat with her, so I waited around to see if he'd leave."

"Did you watch the bedroom window to see if the lights went out?"

"Angela, I don't know if she had a bedroom window. I was never in her house."

"So, I gather he did not leave."

I shook my head and gulped my now-cold coffee.

"Did that piss you off, Tom? That another man who was your inferior was horning in on somebody you cared about?"

I stood up.

"I've had enough of this, Angela. I need to go. Oh, I forgot to tell you that we have a new president. It's Lillian White. Often, in searches, you wind up with only one person after your other finalists withdraw or are rejected. You go with that person or start over. In this case, she is truly the best. I couldn't be happier that we picked a woman of color to take over this place."

"Sit down, Tom. We're not finished."

I sat down in the chair.

"I repeat my question to you: has something happened to Maxine March? It's a simple question. Will you give me a simple answer?"

At that moment, the door to Angela's office opened and two men entered. I jumped to my feet again.

"Who are these guys? I thought this was a private meeting."

"This is Detective Yost and Detective Hardy. You need to go downtown with them right now."

My voice rose to a shout.

"ANGELA, WHAT HAPPENED TO MAXINE MARCH?"

"I'm sorry to tell you that Ms. March's body was found earlier today on the western edge of campus near the covered bridge."

I reacted as if she had hit me in the stomach with a two-by-four. I think I staggered backward a bit before steadying myself on the chair. I know I teared up, despite my efforts at stoicism.

"Maxine's dead? I can't believe it. But why are these guys hovering around me? Her ex-husband's the killer. There's no doubt about that. These guys should go pick up Duncan Delgado, not me. What did you find out about his role in Hector Morales's death and those illegals in the lab?"

"Your faculty ID card was next to the body when we found it. It had blood on it that matches that of Ms. March," she said, ignoring what I said about Delgado.

As I groped for my wallet to show her my card, she nodded to the two detectives. "Gentlemen."

The two men walked up behind me, and one of them — I'm not sure if it was Yost or Hardy — snapped handcuffs on my wrists. The cuffs made a loud clicking noise as he tightened them. Then both of them led me toward the door.

"Somebody set me up, Angela," I yelled over my shoulder. "Somebody set me up."

June 21, 2005

The Benton County Courthouse looked quite different from the other side of the bars. My brain was so numb because of what had happened to me that I could scarcely contemplate my change in circumstances. A little over a year ago, I was in this same courtroom, contemplating my upcoming service on a jury. Now, I was being arraigned for the murder of a woman I did not even know, when I was here before.

Probably because of Angela's intervention, I had been kept in a cell by myself the night before. Although the Benton County Corrections Center was not Attica or San Quentin, someone like me would probably not have fitted in very well with the regular jail population of meth heads and spouse abusers.

Even if my personal safety was not yet at risk, my mental well-being was shot to hell. How would I ever recover my good name?

I was so out of it the night before, I could not even think of an attorney to call. Instead, I used my one allowed phone call to try to reach Paul Bickford. He was the only person I could think of with resourcefulness and connections to get me out of this. Predictably, he was out of the country. The terse message on his voice mail gave no indication as to when he would return.

As a result, I was being represented by a public defender, a young woman who looked like she should be in my freshman news-writing class. She certainly didn't look like she had the ability to defend someone against a murder charge. She was short and a bit on the heavy side, with too much makeup—no doubt to hide the remnants of teenage acne. Her suit made her look even more squat because it was plaid and a bit too tight.

"I haven't had time to read your file yet," she whispered, after I was led into the courtroom, wearing shackles, and slumped down into the seat next to her.

"That's not very comforting," I said, in a sharp tone I regretted as soon as I saw the hurt look in her eyes.

"I'm sorry, but I'm new to all of this. I want to do a good job for you, I really do."

"No, no. I'm the one who should be sorry," I said, patting her arm with my handcuffed hands. "I'm pretty distraught over all of this—and bewildered. Whatever you hear today, I didn't do it. I didn't kill Maxine March!"

I pounded the table with such force that the handcuffs rattled. I glanced around at the deputy standing nearby. He raised an eyebrow, but did not move.

"Sorry," I mouthed in apology.

As the clock struck nine, the door at the rear opened.

"All rise," said the clerk, and she followed the judge into the room. The judge entered at her usual brisk pace, her black robe rustling faintly in the hushed courtroom.

"The circuit court is now in session. The Honorable J. Betty Andrews presiding."

The clerk sat behind her desk on a level lower than the judge and reached over to turn on her computer.

"Please be seated."

"We're here in the matter of arraigning the defendant, Thomas Martindale, for the murder of Maxine March," said Judge Andrews.

As the judge paused for breath, I became aware of the whirring sound of a television camera. As I turned toward the direction of the sound, several still cameras clicked. For the first time, I saw five photographers on my left, as well as three reporters taking notes rapidly. I only recognized the local people, but had no doubt that the others were from Portland. A college professor arrested for anything would be news all over the state. It was too late to worry about the ramifications of the coverage to my career. I was too distracted to contemplate that. All I knew was that everything I had worked for during all the years of my professional life had come to an end. I had no doubt about that.

"I must say the court is surprised to see you here, Mr. Martindale," said the judge, a sadness in her eyes.

I stood up, to clicking camera shutters.

"No more so than I am, Your Honor."

I sat down to more clicking. I was rapidly becoming the victim of a profession I worked in all my life.

"Is the state ready?"

The same rumpled-looking assistant D.A. who had been in the Morales trial got to his feet.

"Yes, Judge. The state charges Thomas Martindale, a 55-year-old male resident of Corvallis, Benton County, Oregon, with the murder of Maxine March, a 55-year-old female resident of Corvallis, Benton County, Oregon."

My mind strayed. So, Maxine had been near my age. I had only guessed before.

"On or about June 19, 2005, the defendant, Thomas Martindale, did cause the death of said Maxine March on or near a covered bridge on the campus of Oregon University, in Corvallis, Benton County, Oregon. The state has presented its evidence to you in the material before you."

"Thank you, Mr. Bates."

"Ms. Scott, how does your client plead?"

When the public defender rose, I stood up with her.

"Not guilty."

Somewhat laughably, we both spoke at the same time, me in a louder voice than the hesitant public defender.

"Given the evidence presented to me, I have no choice but to hold you over for trial, Mr. Martindale. You will remain in custody until bail arrangements can be made."

As I stood there with tears streaming down my face, all I heard was the clicking and whirring of the cameras. When the deputies led me out of the courtroom, I could not hide my despair and the horror of what I was facing. My life—my safe, stimulating, useful, well-paid life—was over.